I0636858

THE QUEENS OF ARMENIA

150 BIOGRAPHIES BASED ON HISTORY AND LEGEND

HAYK KHACHATRIAN

Copyright © 2023 by Hayk Khachatrian

All rights reserved.

No part of this publication may be reproduced, distributed, or
transmitted in any form or by any means, including photocopying,
recording, or other electronic or mechanical methods, without the prior
written permission of the publisher, except as permitted by U.S.
copyright law. For permission requests, contact Yans Press LLC.

Translation by Nouné Sekhpossian, Arpine Ohanyan

Editing by Sydney Rain, Barbara J. Merguerian

Publisher: Yans Press LLC

CONTENTS

QUEENS

KINGDOM OF VAN (URARTU)

AZKANAZIAN/ERVANDIAN DYNASTY

KINGDOM OF TSOPK/COMMAGENE

ARTASHESIAN DYNASTY

ARSHAKUNI DYNASTY

CILICIAN KINGDOM

CREDITS

Special Thanks to
Armenian Apostolic Church

Translation
- Nouné Sekhpossian
- Arpine Ohanyan

Editing
- Sydney Rain
- Barbara J. Merguerian

Illustration
- Artyom Khachatryan

Cover Design
- Narek Yeghiazaryan

Formatting
- Steve Green

Dress Design
- Taraz Art Cultural Center
- Araksya Gabrielyan

Organizing and Help
- Vahe Khachatryan
- Aram Ohanian

Introduction to the Armenian Edition

This book covering women of the Armenian royal court is a continuation of the author's previous work, *Royalty: 141 Armenian Kings*. Understandably, the book does not include foreign queens of Armenian origin. In the Middle Ages, more than one hundred Armenian women became queens of other Christian countries, and scores of them were queens of the Byzantine Empire. They can be called Armenian queens, but not queens of Armenia. We define the queens of Armenia as wives of sovereigns of Armenian state formations, and for that purpose, nationality is not a decisive factor.

Among the 150 queens described in this book, 103 are Armenian, one is Assyrian, eight are Parthian, six are Persian, two are Alan, nine are Greek, six are Roman, four are Georgian, ten are French, and one is Mongol. Wives of all Armenian kings included in *Royalty: 141 Armenian Kings* are presented here. The exception is King Gagik I Bagratuni, who was not married during his reign from 1042 to 1045. He stepped down from the throne at the age of twenty, and later married the daughter of the king of Sebastia, Davit Artsruni.

In the cross sections of history, Armenian queens always supported their husbands and participated in governing, thus helping build prosperity and defend the country. Many Armenian queens did not simply sit solemnly on the throne and enjoy their royal privileges, but showed themselves to be great patriots, sensible, and wise. They carried the burdens of the Armenian state and the Armenian people on their shoulders.

Today, as Armenia has gained its independence and is building its new state foundations under the most difficult conditions, it is necessary to make use of the experience of our ancestors and involve women's wisdom and hard work in that process. At all times, Armenian women demonstrated an independent mind-set and were active and creative members of society. It is not a coincidence that the Armenian goddess of wisdom is a woman, Nané. Nowadays, it is the sacred duty of our statesmen to acknowledge the powerful strength of an Armenian woman's spirit, heart, hands, and mind.

Hayk Khachatrian

1

Introduction to the English Edition

During the early years of Armenia's long existence as a nation, kings ruled the people. But history for the most part has been silent about the women who sat on the throne as royal consorts and influenced—sometime openly, other times subtly—the course of events. Author Hayk Khachatrian has conducted an exhaustive examination of historical sources and legends in order to compile this book containing biographical sketches of all the queens of the Armenians, beginning with the wife of the first sovereign, King Aram, and concluding with Queen Margarita, who ruled with King Levon VI Lusignan until the fall of the last Armenian dynasty in 1375.

On the whole, the author offers a positive image of the queens, presenting them as active helpmates and wise advisors to their royal husbands, loyal, devoted, and often willing to sacrifice luxury for the demands of crown and nation. This is a romantic, even idyllic, view of the relations between queens and their powerful spouses. On the other hand, the author does not hesitate to mention those instances where the queens exhibit selfish, or even treacherous, behavior.

Indeed, we should not be surprised to find a wide range of human emotions on display here: from ambition, pride, courage, and generosity to egotism, vanity, hatred, and cruelty. Unfortunately, the paucity of available information prevents the exploration of human complexities, nor was it the author's intention to dwell on the details of the historical circumstances at play during these many centuries of Armenian history.

We should note that in most of the periods covered in this book, dates are approximate, and considerable controversy among scholars surrounds many of the events and people represented here. The English translation has followed the text of the Armenian edition in these areas.

- Barbara J. Merguerian

SOSEM

The first Armenian who placed a crown on his head and was proclaimed a king was Aram, the son of Harma Nahapet. This happened several thousand years ago, when our generous ancestors counted the centuries by tens. The historian of ancient Armenia, Movses Khorenatsi, believed Armenia gained international recognition as a state formation during the reign of Aram.

History has not preserved the name of Aram's wife, the first Armenian queen. In my unpublished historical novel, I mentioned "King Aram gave her the name of Sosem." I believe this is the most probable name of the first Armenian queen. Sosem gave birth to Ara Geghetsik (Ara the Handsome), one of the most attractive men in the ancient world.

Legend says that young Armenian women tried to meet Queen Sosem and catch her eye, believing an exchange of glances with the mother of Ara the Handsome would assure them of giving birth to a beautiful child. Legend also says that the name Sosem is related to the name of one of the most popular Armenian trees, sosi, or poplar. Unfortunately, the forest of poplar trees in the ancient Armenian capital of Armavir did not survive the passage of time, and we cannot guess from the rustling of its leaves which name gave rise to the other, sosi to Sosem, or Sosem to sosi.

EPIGÉ

The ruler of the kingdom of Ararat, Aramé, reigned from 860 to 840 BC. He battled courageously against the king of Assyria, Salmanasar III, and strengthened and expanded his kingdom. It is not known how many wives King Aramé had, but a story about one of them has survived in Van (Vaspurakan). Here It is.

King Aramé married the beautiful daughter of the richest prince in the city of Van. Her name was Lasma. After becoming queen, Lasma had to renounce her sonorous name and adopt a new one. Aramé said to his wife,

"My Queen, since my young years I have battled the king of Assyria, Salmanasar. He is my worst enemy and I fight with him even in my dreams. When I hear his name, it fills me with rage. I become very irritated when I hear your name, Lasma, because it is composed completely of the same letters as Salmanasar. It seems to me that Salmanasar constructed your name, Lasma, from the letters of his name and sent it to remind me constantly of his existence. Certainly, it is not your fault, it is just coincidence, but one that is unpleasant for me. Let us forget your name. My royal sages have chosen for you the name Epigé. This name does not have any letters from the name Salmanasar. Accept your new name and learn to like it. From now on you will be Queen Epigé for me and for the entire world." This is how the wife of Aramé was named Epigé.

ARKANA

A legend has survived about the second wife of the king of Ararat, Aramé. Her name was Arkana. The first wife of Aramé, Queen Epigé, was not pleased when a second queen appeared at court.

Epigé told her husband, "Aramé, you have been assuring me you had an encompassing love for me."

"That is the truth," confirmed King Aramé.

"Then why did you put the crown on the head of Arkana?"

"Because I want to show the world that I am not only the sovereign of this country, but also its most virile man. All our princes have many mistresses besides the princess. To affirm my omnipotence, and my difference from them, I must have two queens instead of one."

KINGDOM OF VAN (URARTU)

ARARANSA

The founder of the Sarduri dynasty of the kingdom of Van, Sarduri, the son of Lutipri, ruled from 845 to 825 BC. One day, the young Sarduri saw an exquisite girl in the village of Ulunk, in the province of Hayots Dzor, "Valley of the Armenians," and fell in love with her. After some inquiries, he discovered she was the daughter of a common settler. But his love was so strong that he told his father, Lutipri, about it.

"Son, this is not a proper choice for a prince," King Lutipri objected. 'You cannot marry a country girl; you must find a young lady who has an appropriate status."

"But I love that girl and I will not marry another woman."

King Lutipri could not convince his son to abandon his intention. So, he had to issue an edict granting the title of prince to the father of the rural beauty. According to the legend, Lutipri later named[1] the girl Araransa and brought her as a bride for his son. And the wife of Sarduri, Araransa, became the queen.

NAIRA

The king of Van, Ishpuini, inherited the throne from his father, Sarduri and reigned from 825 to 810 BC. Ishpuini loved his native country very much and demonstrated this love at the time of his first marriage. After the wedding, the newlywed queen was carried to the royal palace. Here, according to the tradition of Van, the new queen had to set her foot on the ground and cross the threshold of her husband's home. But Ishpuini's wife refused to step down from the carriage and demanded to be taken into the palace on a sumptuous sedan. Ishpuini was enraged and told her, "If you refuse to set your foot on our sacred land, you are not likely to love this land, this palace, and me after becoming the queen." He ordered the carriage sent back to her father's home. Later Ishpuini married a prince's daughter named Naira, and, according to legend, loved her so much that in his prayers he always mentioned her name first and asked for her happiness.

TARIRIA

The king of Van, Menua, the son and successor of Ishpuini, ruled from 810 to 788 BC. One of the ancient cuneiform inscriptions mentions the name of the daughter of Menua, Tariria. King Menua planted a vineyard for his daughter and named it Tarirakhinele. It was located in Vaspurakan, in the village of Katepants, near the little town of Artamet on the bank of Menua's canal, later renamed Shamiram's canal.

Until 1915, this spot was a favorite place of pilgrimage for Armenians from Van. In the inscription, Menua confirms the vineyard belonged to his daughter, Tariria.

From ancient times up until the fourteenth century, the tradition of naming the first son of the king by the king's name, and the first daughter of the king by the queen's name, continued. Assuming that, according to the tradition, they named Tariria after her mother, we can conclude that the name of Menua's wife was also Tariria.

TILAMA

Inushpua, the son of Menua, reigned from 788 to 786 BC.

An old tale says the name of the wife of Inushpua was Tilama. Queen Tilama manifested genuine kindness to her subjects by suggesting to her husband that they provide royal tax exemptions to the settlers of villages where at least one nurse of the royal infants lived.

BAGENA

The king of Van, Argishti I, second son of Menua, succeeded his brother, King Inushpua, and ruled from 786 to 764 BC. History did not record the name of the wife who ascended to the throne with King Argishti I. But one tale remains in the memory of Armenians from Vaspurakan.

King Menua summoned his seventeen-year-old son, Prince Argishti, and told him, "Tomorrow, the festivities devoted to the gods begin in our capital. All the most beautiful girls from the near and far regions of our country will participate in these festivities. Take a good look at them. The one you like the most will become your bride, the future queen of our kingdom."

The next day Argishti participated in the festivities and looked at the beautiful girls, but did not like any one of them.

"Tell me, which one did you choose?" asked the father at the end of the day of festivities.

"None of them," answered the prince with disappointment.

"Why? Is it possible that not one of the beautiful girls pleased you?" "No, father, there was not one that I liked."

"Son, are you willful or stubborn?" "Neither one nor the other."

"Why then can't you choose a bride?" "I don't know."

"Tomorrow, go again to the festivities and look carefully at the girls," urged King Argishti.

"I doubt I can give a preference to any one of them."

"No, my son, it can't go on like this. You must choose a bride tomorrow. It is not only my paternal demand but also a royal command."

"But what if I cannot choose?"

"Then, do the following," advised the father. "Count the girls and choose the fortieth."

On the next day, following his father's advice, Argishti counted the girls he met at the festivities and stopped at the fortieth.

"What is your name?" asked the prince. "Bagena."

"I like you. You are the most beautiful girl of all."

"How did you determine I am the most beautiful?"

"Because you are the fortieth."

"I don't understand," said Bagena.

"Let's go to my father, and he will explain everything to you," said Prince Argishti, and taking her hand, accompanied her to his father.

Apparently, this was the only case in Armenian history when the queen was chosen based on arithmetic.

SUSARATU

Sarduri II, son and successor of Argishti as king of Van, reigned from 764 to 735 BC. An old tale has survived in Vaspurakan about this king's wife, who was named Susaratu. This splendor-loving queen had the habit of appearing in court wearing a new dress every day. In the capital city of Van, several workshops were occupied with sewing the queen's outfits.

King Sarduri was a wise man. He soon understood the state treasury was emptying from the expenditures on his wife's finery, adornments, and other luxury items. At the same time, royal troops were not armed well enough and did not have the number of chariots for successful battles against the Assyrian army.

Sarduri stripped his wife of the title of queen and ordered her to keep only two dresses for the rest of her life. Then the king spent the wealth in his treasury on armaments, chariots, and supplies for the army. Soon, the army scored victories in battles against the Assyrians.

"If I had tolerated Queen Susaratu's behavior, she would have destroyed my kingdom with her fineries," wrote King Sarduri in his memoirs, which have not survived.

RUSAINA

The son and successor of Sarduri II, King Rusa I of Van, reigned from 735 to 713 BC. We assume the name of his wife was Rusaina. It is possible this was her real name.

Legend says that beauty like that of Rusaina might be found only among goddesses. And King Rusa considered his wife Rusaina a sacred woman.

The wife of Assyria's King Sargon, who lived at the same time, was terribly envious of Rusaina, so much so that she extracted a promise from her husband not only to capture, but to kill, the Armenian queen. Sargon fulfilled his promise to his wife. In the summer of 714 BC, he captured and plundered the temple of Musasir, took all the members of King Rusa's family as prisoners, and ordered Rusaina killed right after entering the temple.

Learning about the horrible death of his adored wife and about the pillage of the temple, Rusa committed suicide.

HASIS

King Argishti II, the son and successor of Rusal, reigned from 718 to 685 BC. An old tale says that the king's wife, Queen Hasis, was the only woman in the world who, within six years, gave birth three times, each time to quadruplet boys, for a total of twelve sons. Argishti was very proud and happy. In honor of those great events, he issued an edict according to which they rewarded all women who gave birth to multiples with twelve silver coins (based on the number of the king's sons) from the royal treasury.

KOTON

The king of Van, Rusa II, son and successor to Argishti, reigned from 685 to 645 BC. The name of Rusa II's wife has not reached us. Legend says that the name of this queen coincided with the most ancient name of the river passing through the present-day capital of Armenia, Yerevan. This river originates from Lake Sevan and flows into the river Eraskh. Its present name is Hrazdan, or Langu.

In the remote past, the river had the name of lidaruni, and earlier it was named Kodon or Koton.[2] In ancient Armenian "don" (or "ton") means water, river, or sea.

The well-known expert in cuneiform, Hovhannes Karageozian, has theorized that five and a half thousand years ago the name of the city of Yerevan was Kodon, taken from the name of the Koton River, meaning "sea river," because it originated from the small sea of Sevan.

In the remote past, the Armenians had a tradition of naming their beloved wives by the names of Armenian rivers. Presumably, by naming his wife Koton, Rusa II expressed his great and passionate love for her.[3]

ORASH

The son and successor of Rusa II, King of Van Sarduri III, reigned from 645 to 635 BC. King Sarduri learned that an extraordinarily beautiful girl lived in the village of Khorgom in the province of Hayots Dzor. The king, accompanied by his suite, went to Khorgom, stopped at the home of the local prince, and met his beautiful daughter, Orash.

Sarduri supposed the girl would agree to marry him without any hesitation. But it turned out otherwise.

"I will agree to marry you only if you outrun me in a contest," said Orash.

The young king grinned and agreed to compete with the girl. In the nearest field, in front of the gathered public, the king and the young lady ran. In the first half of the distance, Orash was ahead of the king, but soon the king passed her and won the competition.

After this competition, the young lady consented to go to the royal court as a bride. But the legend does not end here. The girl kept postponing the wedding.

Finally, one day Sarduri said to her, "Orash, I can see that you hesitate to marry me. You keep postponing our wedding, even though I fulfilled your wish. I ran before the eyes of my countrymen as a mere soldier to please you."

"That is right, you fulfilled my wish, but you did not win the contest." "What do you mean?" asked King Sarduri.

"No, you did not win, but rather I lost. Let us go to a quiet place, far from people's eyes, and you will see you did not win the competition."

They found a suitable place and competed again. This time Orash won.

"Yes, you won, but why didn't you win last time?" asked the king.

"I did not want to win, because the king must be always the winner before the eyes of his subjects."

Sarduri was pleased with the girl's answer and said, "You are not only beautiful but also wise."

In a few days, Orash became the queen.

URANIA

King Sarduri IV of Van, the successor and son of Sarduri III, ruled from 635 to 625 BC. He was a great patriot and a tale about him confirms this.

The capital, Tushpa, was under Assyrian siege, but the defenders of the city bravely resisted the attacks of the enemy. The siege continued for a very long time, and the threat of hunger was real. Panic spread among people. Then a rumor arose that the royal court had abandoned the town through a secret passage and that Sarduri no longer expected to stand against the enemy pressure. This would mean that everyone was on his own.

Some people, in an attempt to save their lives, climbed over the walls of the fortress and tried to run away. Many of them fell into the enemy's hands and were killed.

To stop the panic and to support the patriotic spirit and courage of the people of Tushpa, King Sarduri ordered the queen, their children, and other members of the court to walk in the streets of the town every day to show the citizens that the court had not run away and that Sarduri still believed in a victory. In addition, Queen Urania went to the needy every evening with her maids and servants to bring them food and to support their faith in a final victory.

PATAR

Argishti II, king of Van, the son and successor of Sarduri IV, reigned from 625 to 620 BC. A resident of the village of Kharnurd in the province of Hayots Dzor, whose name Is Sostenes Grigorian, a 1915 genocide survivor, tells a story about Argishti that he heard from his forefathers.

According to that story, King Argishti had a wife by the name of Patar. To prove her devotion to her husband, she always tasted the food served to the king before letting him eat it.

"Why do you act so?" the royal consort was asked.

"I want to prevent any attempt to poison my husband," Queen Patar explained. "Or if that is not possible, let me be poisoned first and leave this world sooner than my royal husband."

TSIRANÉ

The king of Van Erimena, son and successor of Argishti III, reigned from 620 to 610 BC. The wife of Erimina, Queen Isirane, was a dazzling beauty.

Before her marriage, she had the name of Machanuysh after her father.

When she came to the court, King Erimina told his wife, "Forget your name. We have a tradition in the court to change the name of the king's bride to one appropriate for our dynasty."

"And what will be my new name?" asked Machanuysh.

"Tsirane," the king replied. "Tsirani (apricot) is the favorite fruit in our country. Apricot juice is a divine nectar, and that's what our gods drink. They are wiser than humans. They know the apricot is the only fruit worthy of gods. I want you to bring to me, and to our kingdom, the flavor of apricots."

It is said that they carved this tale on a rock near Van, but someone scraped it in 1916. Unfortunately, in our world, many things connected with Armenian history have been wiped out.

HUTSAN

King Rusa I of Van, the successor and son of Erimina, reigned from 610 to 600 BC. Rusa did not keep a harem and was proud of the fact. He always said he did not look at any woman in the world but Queen Hutsan, his only love.

But in a little while, the queen noticed her husband was excessively friendly to her maids of honor. So Hutsan decided to send away all her maids, assuring her husband she did not need them.

One day the queen's mother said, "My daughter, it does not suit the queen to have no maids of honor."

"Mother, court life forced me to let them go. Maids of honor have always served as mistresses for kings and want to keep Rusa from that temptation.

Maybe that is not a tale, but a true story?

KAPUTAN

The king of Van, Rusa IV, son and successor to Rusa III, reigned from 600 to 590 BC. The prince of the village, Kem, in the Armenian province of Vaspurakan had twin daughters, two beautiful girls who resembled each other so much even their mother could not tell them apart. Rumor about the beauty of the sisters reached King Rusa, and the young king went to Kem and took both as his wives.

"I love you both," said the king to his twin wives. "But according to the law, only one of you can become the queen and her eldest son will be the successor to the throne. Decide yourselves which one of you will be named the queen."

"No, Your Majesty, it is better that you decide which one of us will be the queen," said the sisters.

King Rusa pointed to one of them and declared her the queen.

He named her Kaputan. He then said to the other sister, "You will remain a respectable court lady with the name of Bal."

Later on, Rusa distinguished the sisters, Kaputan and Bal, only by the queen's dress. And nobody knows who actually wore the crown. Maybe they put the crown on their heads in turn?

The tale ends here with the exhortation: Always keep twins away from a court.

AZKANAZIAN/ERVANDIAN DYNASTY

ASARHADONIA

Paruyr Skayordi, founder of the Armenian Askanazian kingdom, reigned from 673 to 630 BC. An ally of Assyria, he was married to the daughter of the Assyrian king Asarhadon. Her name was Asarhadonia.

A legend says that on the wedding day, when the procession was approaching the king's palace, the horse harnessed to the bride's chariot neighed. Paruyr Skayordi did not like it, and he unharnessed the horse. Possessing enormous strength, he shouldered the chariot and carried it to the gates of the royal palace.

Nobody before had ever married in such an unusual way. This act of glorifying the bride touched the Assyrian king Asarhadon so much that he added as much silver as the wedding chariot weighed to Asarhadonia's dowry.

TSAMTSAM

The Armenian king Hrachya was the son of Paruyr Skayordi and reigned from 629 to 600 BC. There is no documentary evidence about King Hrachya's wife, but a tale exists about Hrachya's wedding.

On the appointed day, twelve beautiful women from different parts of Armenia gathered in the royal throne room. Every one of them sent affectionate looks to the prince sitting solemnly on the throne. Each woman hoped to be chosen by Prince Hrachya. Luxuriously dressed women stepped out in turn, gracefully passed the prince, and pronounced only one word, the name Hrachya.

After a brief ceremony, Hrachya pointed to the girl named Tsamtsam.

"Why did you choose Tsamtsam? Some of the women were more beautiful than she," the prince was asked.

"I chose the one who pronounced my name most affectionately," answered the prince.

And as it was written in the court records, "A tender voice adds to the beauty of a woman. It makes her more beautiful."

VANUHI

Armenian King Ervand I Sakavakyats reigned from 570 to 560 BC. His wife's name has not come down to us. In my historical novel, *Ervand Sakavakyats*, I named her Vanuhi.

I will keep this fictional name here.

History has preserved the names of two sons of Ervand Sakavakyats and Vanuhi: Tigran and Shavarsh. Tigran was a hunting friend of the Persian king Cyrus [Kyuros], founder of the Achaemenian dynasty. Tigran later succeeded his father and turned Armenia into a powerful kingdom.

The second son, Shavarsh, remained a prince. The famous battlefield of Avarayr, near the Tghmut River, was named Shavarshakan at the time, after him.

A tale says that during the reign of Ervand Sakavakyats, the name of Queen Vanuhi became the symbol of Armenian unity. In each of the forty thousand settlements in Armenia, at least one newborn girl was named Vanuhi after the name of the Armenian capital Van and in honor of King Ervand Sakavakyats and his wife Vanuhi.

After that time, Armenians traditionally gave newborn girls the names of Armenian queens.

ZARUHI

The son of Armenian King Ervand I Sakavakyats, Tigran Ervanduni, succeeded his father on the Armenian throne in 560 and reigned until 535 BC. According to the Armenian historian, Movses Khorenatsi, the name of Tigran Ervanduni's wife was Zaruhi.

In one of the battles, the King Ervand's army suffered a defeat from the Persian army, and the members of the royal court were taken prisoner, even though the king's son Tigran was a hunting friend of the Persian king Cyrus. According to the laws of war, it was necessary to pay a ransom to liberate the Armenians from captivity. Tigran Ervanduni's wife was among the prisoners, and Cyrus asked Tigran how much he would pay in ransom for his wife.

"My own life," answered the prince, looking at his wife.

"I would give up my life, Cyrus, to prevent my wife from ever becoming a servant." [4]

This chivalrous answer is the oldest and most striking illustration of devotion and love for a wife. Recorded by Greek historian Xenophon, we accept it as a historical fact.

This noble expression was pronounced over 2,560 years ago, and it is surprising that it did not enter the textbooks and did not become an example for our youth's education. The ancient Greeks would carve phrases like this on marble for the public to observe. It is incomprehensible why we Armenians do not carve historic dialogue such as this in stone to show the nobility of the Armenian people.

In the history of Movses Khorenatsi, the tale of Tigran and Azhdahak is recorded. The king of Media, whose name was Azhdahak, apprehensive of the strength of the Armenians, became a false friend and ally to King Tigran. Ingratiating himself with the Armenians, he married the sister of King Tigran, Tigranuhi, intending to conspire with her to kill Tigran.

And thus, Tigranuhi came to Erkbatan, the capital of the Median Kingdom, as a bride. Azhdahak tried to convince his Armenian bride that her brother Tigran, at the instigation of his wife, Queen Zaruhi, intended to seize the kingdom of Media and deprive Azhdahak and Tigranuhi of the throne. Tigranuhi guessed the insidious ploy of Azhdahak and kept her brother informed of the plot. Tigran set out against Azhdahak with a large army, liberated his sister, and killed Azhdahak in battle.

Tigran Ervanduni and his wife Zaruhi had three sons—Bab, Tiran, and Vahagn. History does not tell us anything more about Zaruhi, that great Armenian queen. It is known, however, that Tigran Ervanduni and Zaruhi had a long life together filled with a great and enviable love for each other.

TIGRANUHI

Armenian king Hyudarnes, or Hidarnes I Ervanduni, ruled at the end of the sixth century BC. We do not know the name of his wife, the queen of Armenia, but an old tale in Van says that her name was Tigranuhi. In those times, the name Tigran was associated with aristocratic families. The name Tigran also symbolized patriotism. And therefore, the name Tigranuht meant not only the daughter of Tigran, but also a patriotic Armenian woman.

In ancient times Armenian queens were not entitled to issue edicts, but as that old tale relates Tigranuhi was an exception. She issued an edict with the consent of her husband, in which she stated the following, "The wife must bring to her husband's home tenderness and a smile, not just a dowry."

MIHRANA

Armenian King Hyudarnes, or Hidarnes I Ervanduni, ruled at the beginning of the fifth century BC. On the east wall of the central fortress in the ancient capital of Armenia, Armavir, the story of the king's marriage is carved.

Kings of the Ervanduni dynasty were astonishing men. They were very scrupulous about choosing a bride. The future queen would have to possess all the virtues of beauty: a slender waist, fair skin, beautiful neck, delicate nose and lips, a tender look, and straight teeth. Gums should not be in sight when smiling or laughing. It is said that Hyudarnes II Ervanduni compiled these characteristics for a royal bride and had them written in the court rulebook for the purpose of preserving the noble traits of the royal family.

It is probable that his wife, whom we name Mihrana, had all those features, but we know nothing about her life as a queen.

SIPANE

Armenian King Hyudarnes, or Hidarnes III Ervandunt, ruled in the mid-fifth century BC. If we believe an old tale, the name of his wife was Sipané. One day King Hyudarnes, while hunting on the slopes of Mount Sipan, met a beautiful girl who was gathering flowers.

"Where did you come from?" asked Hyudarnes.

"From above," answered the beauty, pointing to the sky. "From the top of the mountain?"

"No, from the sky."

"And where are you going now?"

"I am not going; I am coming to you." "To me?"

19

"Yes."

"What do you want from me?" "I am coming to be your wife."

The tale says that Hyudarnes took the beauty as a gift from heaven, married her, and named her Sipané, because he met her on the slopes of Mount Sipan. Of course, she was not a goddess, and we do not know whose daughter she was to become a queen so quickly.

ASATERA

The Armenian king Artashir Ervanduni reigned in the second half of the fifth century BC. It is said that the name of his wife was Asatera. She had seven sons and married all of them to Armenian women.

As a wise person, Asatera helped her husband govern the kingdom. The following exhortation, believed to originate with Queen Asatera, was carved in the front of Artashir Ervanduni's palace. "Do not take from foreigners either wife or food."

HRODOGUNÉ

King Ervand II Ervanduni ruled from 404 to 360 BC. He married Hrodoguné, the daughter of the Persian king Artaxerxes Mnemon. He rebelled against his father-in-law, Artaxerxes, and fought against him, but later submitted to him and was appointed governor of the province of Troy in Greece.

The only piece of information about this Armenian queen of Persian origin that has reached us is her name. Certain indirect facts, however, confirm that Hrodoguné was a faithful wife.

Ervand II Ervanduni was an uneasy, rebellious person, one of the ancient Armenian mighty warriors. He was in constant conflict with Artaxerxes and continuously strove for independence.

Evidently, Hrodoguné always supported him rather than her father. She was beside him in all his victories and defeats.

TSOVINAR

In the second part of the fourth century BC, King Vahe Ervanduni reigned. It is said that he had a very unruly horse and nobody could straddle it except the king. In 331, after King Vahe's death in the battle of Gaugamela, [5] the soldiers of Alexander the Great attempted to catch the Armenian king's horse, but the horse ran from the battlefield and headed toward Armavir. The next day, the horse reached the Ararat valley, arrived at the capital city, and knocked on the main gate with its hooves.

Learning about the death of her husband, Queen Tsovinar, Vahe Ervanduni's wife, poisoned herself.

"Why did you do it?" a maid of honor asked her.

"Only in this way can I show my devotion to my husband," answered Queen Tsovinar with her last breath.

NANÉ

King Ervand III Ervanduni reigned from 331 to 300 BC. Historical documents do not contain any information about the name of this king's wife. But according to an old tale, the king was a commander in the Persian army in the battles against Alexander the Great, and his beloved wife was beside him in all his marches. We know that Ervand III Ervanduni participated in the battle of Gaugamela in 331 BC, with King Vahé Ervanduni. After the death of King Vahé in that battle, Ervand III became the king of Armenia.

Ervand III Ervanduni liked to say about his wife:

"My queen is not an ordinary woman; she is like the real Nané. She contributed a great deal to my victories in many battles. A wife should be not only a lifelong companion to her husband, she should restrain him from mistakes and failures."

Based on this tale, we can assume that the name of King Ervand III Ervanduni's wife coincided with the name of the Armenian goddess of wisdom, Nané.

We do not know how Nané advised her husband, but evidently, she was an extraordinarily intelligent woman if they compared her to the goddess Nané.

AREG

King Antiochus I Ervanduni left an inscription on Mount Nemrut[6] in the country of Commagene. According to that inscription Ervand III Ervanduni was succeeded by a king whose name ended with "anes." The full name is not known. He reigned from 299 to 270 BC. In my book *Royalty: 141 Armenian Kings*, I named him Vananes and gave his wife a conditional name, Areg

Folktales have no barriers, pass through centuries from generation to generation, and can live as long as a nation lives. A tale remains about Vananes and Areg, according to which Areg always remained awake while her husband was sleeping, thus protecting him from any attempts on his life.

No other queen in the world is known to have been so devoted to her husband.

ERVANDUHI

The last ruler of the Ervanduni dynasty, King Ervand IV, reigned from 220 to 200 BC. He kept a harem and had several wives and mistresses. One of his wives had the title of queen, but we do not know who it was or what her name was. It is known that the Ervandunt dynasty had a tradition whereby, as a sign of love or trust, the new queen put aside the name she brought from her home and took the name of her husband, adding the ending "uhi." Hence, it is possible that according to that tradition the name of King Ervand's wife was Ervanduhi.

We know nothing about the fate of the queen. Did she die a death as cruel as her husband's[7] or did she live a peaceful and long life? We cannot answer.

KINGDOM OF TSOPK/COMMAGENE

SAMOSIA

Samos Ervanduni was the founder of the Armenian Ervanduni kingdom of Tsopk-Commagene and reigned in the middle of the third century BC. A tale says that, as was usual in the Ervanduni dynasty, the name of the king's wife was Samosia, based on her husband's name.

This Armenian queen had the habit of examining and evaluating samples of items of luxury and adornment made in the workshops of the capital city of Samosat.

Only after her approval were the luxury items produced.

HIERAKSIA

Hrsham Ervanduni, the successor of the founder of the Armenian Ervanduni kingdom of Tsopk-Commagene, Samos, ruled from 240 to 220 BC. Arsham was an ally of the Seleucid king, King Seleucus II's brother, Antiochus Hieraks, who intended to weaken the Seleucid Kingdom.

It is probable that the marriage of Arsham to the daughter of Antiochus Hieraks, Hieraksia, strengthened the alliance.

There is no historic evidence about how this Hellenic woman reigned as an Armenian queen.

ANTIOCHIA

The king of the Armenian kingdom of Tsopk-Commagene, Xerxes Ervanduni, followed his father Arsham to the throne and ruled during the last half of the third century BC.

At the beginning of his reign, Xerxes rebelled against the Seleucid Antiochus III the Great, but later became reconciled with him and married his sister Antiochia (or Antiochis).

The Seleucid ruler, however, discovering that he could not completely subdue

Xerxes, subsequently organized a plot against him, taking advantage of his sister's position. This Hellenic woman, who carried the name of the Antiochus dynasty, betrayed her husband after becoming the Armenian queen.

These events are described by the Greek historian Polybius (third century BC) in the Eighth Book of his history:

"During the reign of Xerxes, King Antiochus besieged the town of Armosata,[8] which was between the Euphrates and Tigris rivers in the so-called Beautiful Field.[9] Xerxes at first attempted to escape, but the fall of the capital city would have meant the loss of the entire kingdom, and therefore he asked Antiochus to negotiate.

"Some of the faithful friends of Antiochus advised him not to let Xerxes out of the town, but to capture the capital and to transfer power to his cousin Mihrdat. [10] But Antiochus did not follow their advice and invited the young man to his quarters. He reconciled with him and even forgave a big part of his father's debt. Afterwards, upon receiving from Xerxes three hundred talents, one thousand horses, and one thousand mules, Antiochus returned all authority to him and married him to his sister, Antiochia."[11]

According to Polybius, this marriage of Xerxes Ervanduni and Antiochia took place in 212 BC. Antiochus III the Great gave as a dowry to Xerxes several Armenian provinces under his control.

However, the Armenian king could not tolerate a longtime dependence on the Seleucid king, and sometime after the reconciliation described above, he rebelled once again. Realizing that Xerxes Ervanduni could not be totally subjugated, this time Antiochus III the Great plotted against him. With the help of his sister, the Armenian queen Antiochia, he had Xerxes Ervanduni assassinated. This happened sometime between the years 215 and 200 BC. It may be supposed that Queen Antiochia, carrying out her brother's instructions, poisoned her husband.

ASTGHIK

Zareh Ervanduni was the commander in Tsopk from 202 to 201 BC, and the king of Tsopk from 190 to 175 BC. A tale relates that Zareh's wife was a Hellenic woman by the name of Melea, which means "water nymph" in Greek.

When Zareh became king, he asked his wife, "Are you glad to be a queen?"

"Yes, of course I am," replied Melea.[12]

"And I would be glad if we changed your name." "But why don't you like my name?"

"Your name is very melodious, but it does not sound Armenian enough for an Armenian queen."

"And what would you like to call me?"

"Astghik. That is the name of the Armenian goddess of love and beauty."

"I agree. Everyone would like to be called by the name of the goddess of beauty." And thus, the wife of Zareh assumed the name of Queen Astghik.

LUSATIKIN

The son of Zareh, Arkatias Ervandni, succeeded his father as king of Tsopk and reigned in the second century BC.

According to an old tale, his wife's name was Lusatikin.

Lusatikin was a brave woman. Learning about the death of her husband, she took command of the Armenian army, courageously battled against Seleucid King Antiochus IV Epipanes, and drove his army out of the Armenian kingdom.

That was vengeance for the death of her husband.

HUTOMIA

The king of Tsopk, Arkatias Ervanduni, was succeeded by his brother from Gamirk, Mehruzhan Ervanduni, who ruled in the second century BC. The tale says that he loved his wife Hutomia so much that he issued an order according to which all men of the kingdom, including himself and the princes, were prohibited from keeping mistresses.

MORCH

Artashes Ervanduni succeeded Mehruzhan as king of Tsopk and reigned from the end of the second century to 94 BC. The name of the king's wife was Turasamiaramorch, but the king did not like it.

"My queen, your name is too long and unsuitable for a queen. Let us shorten it and call you by the last part of your name only, Morch."[13]

And the wife of King Artashes Ervanduni was known to the world as Queen Morch. Everything else about her life is covered by the darkness of past centuries.

ASPANUYSH

Reigning in Commagene from the end of the third century to the beginning of the second century BC was Armenian King Ptghomeos Ptolemy Ervanduni.

The real name of his wife is not known, and we will call her Aspanuysh. This beautiful woman had extraordinarily white skin and did not keep any maids of honor.

"My king, I always keep my skin out of the view of people. I always dress appropriately and don't keep maids, so they don't see my skin. Otherwise, learning about the extraordinary whiteness of my body, the kings of neighboring kingdoms would go to war against you."

"Oh yes, you are right. A beautiful wife resembles an estate, and it is necessary to defend it by all means," said King Ptolemy Ervanduni.

ARTASA

Armenian King Samos II Ervanduni reigned in Commagene in the second century BC. According to a tale, his wife's name was Artasa. They only had one child, a beautiful daughter whose caprices and wishes they fulfilled unreservedly.

The princess fell in love with a Greek prince and married him.

The king gave her a large dowry, including seven villages near the town of Samosat which had been part of the dowry of his wife Artasa. Queen Artasa opposed this decision of the king because she did not want these Armenian villages to be transferred to the control of Greeks.

"My darling," said Artasa to her husband, "it is not a good idea to give a dowry as a new dowry."

But the king did not follow his wife's advice, and this had very serious consequences.

It so happened that the king's daughter died suddenly, and sometime later the son-in-law married a Greek princess. The princess brought several Greek families with her to the Armenian lands, and these Greeks forced the Armenians out of their seven native villages.

King Samos, realizing that his former son-in-law was becoming a dangerous enemy, asked him to abandon the Armenian villages.

However, the Greek ridiculed him and showed him the document, confirming the receipt of those villages as a gift in perpetual possession. Then King Samos used military force against the Greeks and drove them out of the Armenian lands.

After this incident, Samos II Ervanduni left a bequest to his descendants: "Never give land as a dowry."

ARSHANVYSH

The Armenian King Mihrdat Kalinikos Ervandunt ruled in Commagene in the second century BC. A tale says that the name of Mihrdat Ervanduni's wife was Arshanvsh.

When Arshanvysh entered the royal court, she learned that the former wife of the king had been a very garrulous woman, to such a degree that she impeded the king's rule of the kingdom.

The court councilors had concluded that garrulity was an incurable human shortcoming, and in the case of a king or a queen, it could become a cause for the entire kingdom's downfall. Mihrdat Kalinikos had been obliged to divorce her.

Learning about this, Arshanvysh was very careful not to speak too much. In fact, she spoke so rarely that her husband once said to her, "Arshanvysh, do not be so taciturn. People will think that you are deaf."

VOSKEMAYR

Armenian King Antiochus I Ervanduni ruled in Commagene from 69 to 3＝ BC. In an ancient inscription on Mount Nemrut in Commagene, King Antiochus I wrote that he was a direct descendent of Ervand II Ervanduni and the daughter of Artaxerxes, the Achaemenian Hrodoguné.

In the row of goddesses on Mount Nemrut stands, among others, the statue of the Armenian goddess of maternity, Voskemayr "Golden Mother" Anahit. It can be supposed that this statue represents not only the goddess but also the wife of Antiochus\Ervanduni, whose name had not reached us. We will call her Voskemayr, according to one name given to the goddess Anahit. The queen was an Armenian woman. It is also quite possible that she was a daughter of Tigran II the Great.

HAYAMA

In the first century BC, Armenian King Antiochus IV Ervanduni reigned in Commagene. His wife's name was Hayama. A tale says that this extraordinarily beautiful queen liked to swim for hours in the local rivers and lakes.

There is a legend about the goddess Astghik, who liked to bathe in the river at the base of Mount Grgur. She filled the nearest slopes with fog to hide her beautiful body from the eyes of strangers. King Antiochus could not fill with fog the area where his wife swam, so he formed a special unit of his bodyguards to block all the roads to that area.

ARTASHESIAN DYNASTY

SATENIK

Artashes I the Good was the founder of the Artashesian royal dynasty and reigned from 189 to 160 BC. In his history, Movses Khorenatsi cites a legend about the marriage of King Artashes I the Good to Satenik, daughter of the king of the Alans. This legend, called "Artashes and Satenik" and written by the troubadours of Goghtan, presents an excellent example of ancient Armenian literature. The Alans were the ancestors of the contemporary Northern Caucasian nation of Ossetia.

According to the legend, the Alan army invaded Armenia, but was defeated and retreated beyond the Kura River. The king of the Alans asked for peace and offered a large ransom for his son, who the Armenians had captured. Artashes refused the request.

But then he caught sight of Satenik, the Alan king's daughter, standing on the other side of the river. He fell in love with her and kidnapped her. He mounted his horse, crossed the river, threw his strap around her waist, and brought her back to his army. The entire legend is written in rhymed, poetic form. Here are some lines:

Noble King Artashes mounted a beautiful black horse, and taking a strap of red leather with golden rings and crossing the river like a swift-winged eagle and throwing the strap of red leather with golden rings he cast it around the waist of the Alan princess, greatly paining the tender maiden's waist: and he quickly brought her to his camp.

A magnificent royal wedding followed. Again, according to the troubadours.

A shower of gold rained down at the marriage of Artashes; it rained pearls at the wedding of Satenik.[14]

Movses Khorenatsi writes that King Artashes I and Satenik had six sons: Artavazd, Vruyr, Mazhan, Zareh, Tiran, and Tigran.

DSHKHO

Artavazd, the first son of King Artashes I the Good, succeeded his father and reigned from 160 to 115 BC. A tale says that King Artavazd chose one woman from his harem, made her the queen, and named her Dshkho, which means "queen" in ancient Armenian.

But Queen Dshkho could not give birth to a child and the king rejected her. Then he chose seven other beautiful women and promised that the one who gave birth to a son would become the queen.

"If all of you give birth to boys, all of you will become queens," he said.[15]

Legend holds, however, that despite all his efforts, Artavazd never had a son, and none of these women ever became queen.

ANAHIT

Tigran I, son of Artashes I, succeeded his brother Artavazd I and reigned from 115 to 95 BC. The name of his wife is not known. In my historic novel *Tigranes the Great*, I named her Eranuhi, but here I will name her Anahit, according to the name of the Armenian goddess of maternity.

We don't know anything about this queen, except that she gave birth to a son who would become the greatest person in Armenian history, King Tigran II the Great.

For that alone, Anahit deserves eternal recognition. She experienced both happiness and suffering through King Tigran. She suffered from longing, because for over fifteen years her son was a hostage in the Parthian world. And she was happy when her son, after he became the king, turned Armenia into one of the most powerful kingdoms of that period.

Legend says that Tigran II buried his mother in an unattractive cave near the summit of Mount Ararat, which at the time was not covered with everlasting snow. Evidently, the king made sure that the grave remained in an unknown place so that no one would plunder it.

HUTOMIA

King of kings, Tigran II the Great, lived for eighty-five years and reigned from 95 to 55 BC. He ascended the throne when he was forty-five years old, and during the following forty years led Armenia to the apex of its power. The ancient historian Velleius Paterculus named King Tigran II the greatest king of the century. During the reign of Tigran I, Greater Armenia became the second most powerful kingdom in the world.

Like all the rulers of those times, Tigran the Great had a harem of wives and mistresses. According to the tradition of those times, he named one wife the queen, and her children received the right of succession to the throne. Tigran the Great had four queens, not just one. One queen was named Hutomia.

At the end of the second century BC, before Tigran II ascended the throne, the Parthian king Mihrdat [Mithradates] II invaded Armenia with his army and defeated King Artavazd I. The Armenians had to cede to the Parthians the southeastern provinces of Armenia with their seventy valleys and to give up the king's nephew, Prince Tigran (son of Tigran I and the future Tigran the Great) as hostage. Because of his uncle's defeat, Tigran spent fifteen years of his life as a hostage in two Parthian capitals—in the city of one hundred gates, Hekatompilos, and in the famous Erkbatan.

The Parthian king of kings Mithradates II married the Armenian heir to the throne, as a guarantee of dependence, to an aristocratic Parthian woman named Hutomia.[16] In Parthia, Hutomia, who had never seen Armenia, was called the queen of Armenia, and her daughter by Tigran was married to King Mithradates II. In other words, Mithradates II became the son-in-law of his hostage, Tigran! We assume that this daughter of Tigran was named Hutomia, after her mother, but Vardan Hatsuni has assumed her name to be Tigranadukht.[17] By the way, Tigran's daughter was Mithradates II's third wife. The first two were his half-sisters (on his father's side), Siaké and Azaté.

We don't know much about this wife of Tigran the Great.

Hutomia became a real queen of Armenia when Tigran returned to his homeland and became king in 95 BC.

CLEOPATRA

In 94 BC, Tigran the Great entered an alliance with the King of Pontus Mithradates VI Eupator. The ancient historian Hustinos asserted that this alliance was cemented by the marriage of Tigran II to the daughter of Mithradates, Cleopatra. At the time, Tigran was forty-seven years old, and Cleopatra was only sixteen. This girl, thirty-one years younger than Tigran, played a decisive role not only in the life of Tigran the Great, but in the interrelations between kingdoms with connections to Armenia.

Cleopatra is a Greek word which means "glory"— "fame"—of the father. Mithradates's daughter Cleopatra completely justified her name, as she devoted her life and actions to increase the glory of her father. Having been raised and educated in the Pontus court in a Hellenic culture, she surrounded herself in the Armenian court with prominent Greek figures. This beautiful woman was a loyal daughter of her father and very proud of her origin. Mithradates Eupator was a descendent of Cyrus and Darius on his father's side, and of Alexander the Great on his mother's side. As an Armenian queen, Cleopatra remained a faithful ally of Mithradates Eupator.

Mithradates Eupator, like the powerful Carthaginian general Hannibal, was a sworn enemy of Rome and had battled against the Romans his entire life. His aim was to unite as many allies as possible on his side, and Armenia was one of them.

Cleopatra married Tigran with precisely this aim. But Tigran the Great was a more sensible ruler than Mithradates Eupator and never allowed the king of Pontus to manipulate him.

Tigran and Cleopatra had three sons. They named the oldest Zareh and the youngest, Tigran; we don't know the name of the middle brother. All three sons betrayed their father. In this betrayal, Mithradates Eupator played his part. At first Cleopatra did everything to convince King Tigran to conclude an Armenia-Pontus alliance against Rome. However, she failed. The Armenian king followed an independent foreign policy based on the interests of his nation.

Then the king of Pontus tried to put his grandsons on the Armenian throne to have them as allies against the Rome. Cleopatra's sons then attempted to seize the throne before their time had come. Their father executed both the first and second sons. The king also did not forgive the treachery of his youngest son, Tigran.

Cleopatra, under the influence of her father, instigated her sons to betray their father, which caused King Tigran much pain. In 66 BC, when the Roman commander Pompey captured the youngest son and took him to Rome as a hostage, Cleopatra left Armenia and returned to her father, to Pontus, where she lived for the rest of her life.

HAMASPYUR

We don't know the name of the third wife of Tigran the Great. In my historical novel *Tigran the Great*, I named her Hamaspyur; let us keep that fictional name here as well. Hamaspyur gave birth to the successor to the throne, son of Tigran the Great, Artavazd I.

We know nothing else about Hamaspyur, including how many other children she had. She certainly felt animosity toward Queen Cleopatra. Each queen wanted to see her son on the throne, and this led to rivalry and hostility among them. In his lifetime, Tigran the Great designated Artavazd as his lawful successor.

SOSEM-ZOSIMA

The name of the fourth wife of Tigran the Great was Sosem. This name in the Greek language sounds like Losima, and the ancient world knew this Armenian queen by that name. The Roman commander Pompey captured her, took her to Rome, and put her on display in September of the year 61 BC during the celebration of his victory on the field of Mars. H. H. Chakmakjian uses the name Sosem for this queen. [18] Hrand K. Armen writes that the successor of Tigran the Great, Artavazd, was "probably" the son of Queen Zosima.[18] However, this is quite unlikely. Pompey would not have captured the mother of Artavazd when Armenia and Rome were concluding a peace treaty in Artashat in 66 BC. By the way, Artavazd signed that treaty as well, and if Zosima had been his mother, then the father and son pair would have brought her home with no problem.

Not everything was recorded in the original historic sources. But one story has reached us as a legend. In 70 BC, the princes of the town of Baghesh (Bitlis) gathered to decide the destiny of an extraordinarily beautiful seventeen-year-old daughter of one of them, named Sosem. She was not only very beautiful, but also extraordinarily tall. Her height was four kangun (over six feet, eight inches). [19]

In those times, Sosem was the tallest woman in Asia. Her beauty and height attracted the attention of so many high-born suitors that the princes of Baghesh could not decide on her groom. Finally, it was suggested that only King Tigran the Great deserved to have Sosem as his wife. And thus, this tall beauty became one of the four Armenian queens of this ruler. Tigran did not have any children with her.

Under unclear circumstances, the Roman legionnaires of Gnaeus Pompey captured her along with her maid of honor and, undoubtedly secretly from King Tigran, took her to Rome as a captive. One can imagine the arrogance with which they displayed her in Rome at the celebration of Pompey's victory on the field of Mars.

"Dear Romans, look carefully at this tall woman. She is beautiful, isn't she? And she is the tallest woman in the world! Pass your eyes over her fluttering jewelry. And let it be known that this beauty is Zosima, one of the wives of the king of kings of the Armenians, Tigran."

After pronouncing these words, there would have been a moment of silence, during which a strong exclamation of admiration would have been heard, along with words glorifying Pompey.

These celebrations in Rome, taking place on the field of Mars, were cruel exhibitions, designed to abase the defeated. As to how Pompey treated Sosem after the celebration, we have no information. We relate the name Sosem to the name of the poplar tree (sosi). It was the favorite tree in pagan Armenia, and that's why a female name originated from it.

Why have Armenians forgotten that beautiful ancient name? Alas, nowadays many Armenian beauties are called by foreign names awkward to the Armenian language. Let us hope that this tender ancient name will come back.

ZAHANIRA

Tigran, the youngest son of Tigran the Great and Cleopatra, was the vice-king of Tsopk from 69 to 66 BC.

Then he was captured by Pompey and taken to Rome, where they killed him in 58 BC.

This betrayer of his father had a stormy life. In 67 BC, he married the daughter of the Parthian King Hrahat III. Her name is unknown, but in my historic novel *Artavazd,* I called her Zahanira.

This Parthian woman shared all the difficulties of her husband's life, filled with unexpected events. During the celebration of Pompey's victory on the field of Mars in 61 BC, Tigran, his wife Zahanira, and their young daughter were also showed as the Armenian king of kings and the queen of Armenia, although they had never held those titles.

This event was recorded historically. Dio Cassius[20] wrote that Pompey called the captured Tigran "the Armenian king of kings" during the celebration of his victory in Rome, contrary to accepted rules. [19]

Zahanira and her daughter lived in Rome until the death of Tigran in 55 BC. Their fate after his death is unknown.

ARAKSA

The Armenian king Artavazd II, son of Tigran the Great, reigned from 55 to 34 BC. He was also known as a playwright. The name of his wife has not reached us. In my historical novel *Artavazd,* I called her by a fictional name, Araksa. Artavazd II was captured—during the Roman civil war by Marc Antony—and taken with his family to Alexandria, Egypt. His queen, an extraordinarily beautiful woman, shared all the torments that became her husband's lot. Legend says that the famous queen of Egypt Cleopatra once asked the Armenian king Artavazd II, "Who is the most beautiful woman in the world?"

"My wife," answered Artavazd.

Maybe this answer explains why Cleopatra ordered Artavazd to be beheaded. Probably, like Ara the Handsome, Artavazd loved his wife so much that he never had a harem, unlike all the other rulers of those times.

It is also probable that, after the death of Artavazd, Araksa and her sons were taken to Rome under the mercy of the Roman Emperor Augustus. Later, when her son Tigran III became the king of Armenia, Araksa returned to her homeland and died in Artashat.

After her return to the Armenian capital, Araksa went to the banks of the Eraskh River every day and walked on the Taper Bridge, remembering her husband, who was a true king, not only by right of succession but also as a very handsome man of high dignity. It is said that during one of those walks she was so immersed in her memories that she lost her balance, fell off the bridge, and drowned in the whirlpools of the river.

SASA

Artashes II, who had escaped when his family was taken captive, concluded a military alliance with the Parthian King Hrahat IV in 30 BC and, with his help, ascended the throne of his father, King Artavazd II, who had been killed in Alexandria.[21] King Artashes II reigned from 30 to 20 BC. According to the customs of those times, he kept a harem. Apparently, two of his wives were called queens. One of them was Armenian, and the other one was Parthian.

The name of the Armenian wife of Artashes was probably Sasa.

She was very beautiful. Legend says that, after the tragic death of her husband, many princes offered to marry Sasa, but she remained faithful to Artashes II and later poisoned herself to escape the pursuits of these men.

JANAMA

A marriage usually sealed alliances such as that between Armenia and Parthia. The historian Hand K. Armen writes: "In ancient times it was an honorable custom to confirm a political alliance by a marriage. The bride was something more important than the royal stamp on the pact."[22]   One can say with confidence that Artashes II married the daughter of the Parthian king, Hrahat IV. We will call her Janama.

For ten years, from 30 to 20 BC, Janama was the Armenian queen. After the death of Artashes II, Janama did not leave Armenia, and as legend says, did not remarry. Like Sasa, Janama remained faithful to her husband and died on his grave.

OCTAVA

The younger son of King Artavazd, Tigran III, succeeded his brother Artashes II and reigned from 20 to 8 BC. He was brought up in the Roman court of the Emperor Gaius Octavian (Augustus).

Most probably, Tigran III married the daughter of Emperor Octavian, whom we conditionally call Octava. However, neither the influence of Octavian nor the marriage to his daughter prevented Tigran III from ruling Armenia independently. The wife of Tigran III, the queen of Armenia, had always been faithful to her husband and never betrayed him, as the following tale confirms. In those times, the men close to Emperor Augustus often visited the Armenian capital, Artashat.

However, they did not bring any good news to the emperor.

"What did my daughter Octava say?" asked Augustus to a Roman who had just returned from Artashat.

"She said she was very happy to be the Armenian queen.

"Did you not tell her that her husband forgot all his years in Rome and ignores me, the emperor?"

"I told her, but for her, the most important thing is Tigran's love."

"Alas! I should have educated my daughter and not the Armenian prince Tigran," concluded Emperor Augustus.

ERATO

In the centuries before Christianity, incestuous marriages were frequent in the Armenian court. The purpose of such marriages was to preserve the purity of the royal blood, though it is now known that such marriages often produce unhealthy offspring.

According to this custom, the son of Armenian king Tigran III, Tigran IV, married his half-sister, Erato. The historian Hrand K. Armen supposes that Tigran IV and Erato had different mothers.[23] The classical historian Tacitus wrote in the second book of his work *Annals*: "Neither King Tigran, nor his children, reigned long, though the latter according to foreign (not Roman) custom married each other in order to rule together."[24]

Erato, together with her brother Tigran IV, reigned from 8 to 5 BC, from 2 BC to AD 2, and later from AD 6 to 11. She was the last representative on the throne of the Artashesian royal dynasty. The Roman Emperor Augustus appointed Artavazd III as the king of Armenia in 5 BC. However, the Armenians rebelled against Artavazd and restored Tigran I and Erato to the throne. Queen Erato reigned until AD 11.

Erato was the only one among 141 Armenian sovereigns to ascend the throne three times. Following an old custom, they named her Erato, one of the nine muses of the ancient Greeks, the muse of love songs. In short, Erato means love.

The queen was once asked: "Have you enjoyed in your life the kind of love worthy of your name?"

"No," she replied. "I was known to the world as a woman named Erato, but I carried on my shoulders a load suitable for seven men."

HARMONIA

We do not know the name of the wife of King Artavazd I, who reigned from 5 to 2 BC. He was the son of King Artavazd II. We may call her by the name of Harmonia, the daughter of the Greek gods Ares and Aphrodite, because she was very proud of the harmony of her body.

This Armenian queen, Roman by origin, never meddled in the affairs of the kingdom and was occupied mainly with multiplying her adornments and wealth. When she was fleeing from the country, the Armenians set two of her carriages filled with adornments and clothes on fire.

ARSHAKADUKHT

Ancient Armenian historians contend Vagharshak was the brother of Parthia's King Arshak the Great, or Mihrdat I the Great, and with his help reigned in Armenia for thirty-one years in the second century.

We do not know the name of his wife, and will call her Arshakadukht. Legend says that Vagharshak and Arshakadukht had ascetic eating habits; they ate very little, even during big feasts, and never dined after sunset. They considered this a fundamental condition of longevity, and they were never sick during their entire lives.

ANUYSH

From AD 4 to 5, Artavazd IV, son of the king of Atrpatakan, Gaius Octavian Ariobarzan, reigned as king of Atrpatakan and Greater Armenia. The Armenians killed this Roman protégé.

Artavazd had a harem and designated one of those women as the queen of Atrpatakan. When she came to Armenia with her husband, she also wanted to become the queen of Armenia. And although the Armenians never officially recognized either King Artavazd or his wife, Anuysh, she was the de facto queen of Armenia for two years.

Legend says that the Armenians killed their alien king, probably Artavazd IV, but did not harm his wife. Rather, they put her in a royal carriage and escorted her to the Armenian border.

ELECTRA

Armenian King Tigran V reigned for only a few of months after he ascended the throne with the help of Roman Emperor Augustus in AD 6. His father Alexander was the son of the King of Israel Herovdes I, and his mother Glaphyura (Artashesian on her mother's side) was the daughter of King Arkelaos of Gamirk- Cappadocia.

The name of King Tigran V's wife, who became the Armenian queen for a few months, has not come down to us. According to one old tale, her name was Electra.[25] By origin, half Greek and half Roman, she was a very vain woman. For most of her life she lived in Rome, but she liked to wear a mantle with the bright inscription "Electra, Queen of the Armenians," provoking the smiles of the Romans.

BAGARATUHI

King Zeno-Artashes was not Armenian by origin, but Armenians recognized him as their king and loved him.

He reigned from AD 18 to 34.

Legend says that Zeno-Artashes's wife was named Bagaratuhi, and she was a daughter of one of the prominent princes of the Armenian capital, Artashat. She was a lover of education and a kind-hearted woman who always helped her needy but hard-working subjects. However, she did not like lazy people!

ARSHAKUNI DYNASTY

SHAHASPDUKHT

Armenian King Arshak I was the son of the Parthian King Artavazd II and reigned from AD 34 to 35. The wife of King Arshak I, Shahaspdukht was Parthian. An old tale says that in only one year, with the help of her maids of honor, Shahaspdukht learned the Armenian language so well that she was taken for a native Armenian. After the death of her husband, she returned to Parthia, now turned into an Armenian.

ZENOBIA

Mihrdat the Iberian reigned in Armenia from AD 35 to 37 and from AD 47 to 51. He was the brother of Pharsman, king of neighboring Iberia (present-day Georgia). At the same time, he was married to his niece, his brother Pharsman's daughter, Zenobia.[26] And the son of Pharsman, Hradamizd, was married to the daughter of Mihrdat the Iberian and Zenobia.

This Armenian queen of Georgian origin, Zenobia, suffered a tragic fate. In AD 51, Mihrdat's nephew and Queen Zenobia's brother, Hradamizd, invaded Armenia with a large army, determined to seize the Armenian throne. Mihrdat, Zenobia, and other members of the royal family were at in the impregnable fortress of Garni the time, which Roman legions defended.

Hradamizd bribed the Roman prefect [Caelius] Pollio, and under the pretense of an armistice called Mihrdat out of the fortress, embraced him, and promised not to use violence against him: neither sword nor poison. Hradamizd apparently remembered his promise and did not use the sword or poison against his uncle and his sister. Instead, he smothered Mihrdat under heavy carpets, then ordered Mihrdat's wife—his own sister—the Armenian queen Zenobia, and their children to be murdered.[27]

MAYA

For two years, from AD 37 to 38, Kotis, cousin of the king of Greater Armenia, Zeno-Artashes, ruled Armenia.

According to a tale, Kotis married a woman named Maya, who was the niece of the Roman Emperor Caligulla.

Maya is the name of the Greek goddess of the fields, the daughter of Atlas and the mother of Hermes. But despite her name, this Roman woman had nothing divine about her. Not only did she not care for fields and the peasants who worked the soil, but she convinced King Kotis to raise their taxes. The tale says nothing else about her.

ZENOBIA

In the period from AD 51 to 53, Hradamizd, son of the king of neighboring Iberia Pharman and his second wife, Dadana, reigned in Armenia. Hradamid married the daughter of Mihrdat the Iberian, Zenobia. She was the queen of Armenia for about two or three years.

When the future king Trdat entered Armenia, Hradamizd had to step down from the throne and flee the country. The historian Tacitus, in Book 12, Section 51 of his work *Annals*, writes:

"Swift horses were all that saved Radamist (Hradamizd). They carried him and his wife away. But she was pregnant. At first, she endured the journey as best she could, for terror of her enemies and love of her husband. But the continuous

galloping soon shook and jarred her so terribly that she begged to be rescued from the humiliations of captivity by an honorable death.

"Radamist admired her courage: sick with fear of leaving her to someone else, he embraced, comforted, and encouraged her.

"But he was a man of violence; and finally, in the vehemence of his love, he drew his saber, stabbed her, dragged her to the bank of the Arax River, and hurled her in, so that not even her corpse should be taken. Then he rode full speed to his own land of Iberia (Georgia).

"But Zenobia was found by shepherds in a backwater. She lived; she was still breathing. Concluding from her noble appearance that she was someone distinguished, they bandaged her wound and applied rustic remedies. When they learned her name and story, they took her to the city of Artaxata (Artashat). From there she was officially conducted to King Trdat, who received her kindly and gave her royal honors." [28]

Historic sources say that Zenobia soon gave birth to a son who later reigned in Iberia as King Pharsman II (from AD 100 to 114). According to the historian Leo, Zenobia lived in Trat's court until her death.

Zenobia's life, full of adventure, became the subject of novels by two European authors, Kriftlon(e) (1674–1762) and Metastazio (1698–1782). The work of the latter was translated into the Armenian language by Eduard Hyurmyuzian, a member of the Mkhitarist Order in Venice. [28]

BAKURADUKHT

Trdat I Arshakuni, son of the first Arshakuni king of Parthia, Vrnon II, and the youngest brother of King Vagharshak of Parthia and King Bakur of Atrpatakan, reigned in Armenia from AD 52 (officially from 66) to 75.

An ancient tale says Trdat I Arshakuni kept a large harem.

Two women from the harem were queens—a woman of Parthian origin, Bakuradukht, and an Armenian woman, Chermakuhi. Those women held each other in high respect. This was the only pair of Armenian queens who passed their lives in peace with each other. Bakuradukht learned the Armenian language, and Chermakuhi learned Parthian.

CHERMAKUHI

The name of the second wife of the Armenian king Trdat I Arshakuni was Chermakuhi[29]. The king married this Armenian woman after he ascended the Armenian throne in AD 66.

Chermakuhi was from a noted aristocratic family. Considering Chermakuhi meant "white woman" in the Armenian language, King Trdat I Arshakuni did not change her name. The tale says that neither the sons of Chermakuhi, nor the sons of the first queen Bakuradukht, ascended the throne.

CAPITOLA

In AD 60–61, King Tigran VI, son of Alexander and brother of the Armenian King Tigran V, ruled Armenia. The name of Tigran VI's wife is not known. Apparently, she was Roman and probably a daughter of someone from Emperor Nero's court. We will assume her name was Capitola after the name of the highest of the seven hills of ancient Rome, Capitoline, where her father's home was located.

Capitola did not like the Armenian capital of Artashat, and she moved out of Armenia before her husband left.

"Armenia is a land of exaggerations," said Capitola. "It is impossible to live in Artashat, where the cold is exceptionally cold, and the heat is unbearably hot. They don't get mixed together, to moderate each other. The Armenians also are people of exaggerations—they are never satisfied by the good, they want the best."

SANDUKHT

Armenian King Sanatruk Arshakuni succeeded Trdat I and reigned from AD 75 to 110. Both praise and criticism have been used to describe Sanatruk. Ancient historian Arianos writes: "Armenian King Sanatruk was a man of medium height, but he liked big actions, especially military operations. He was a faithful defender of justice, had a moderate lifestyle, and was a sensible man, like the best among the Greeks and Romans."

Armenian historian Moves Khorenatsi writes that, at thirty, Sanatruk was killed accidentally by an arrow while hunting, "as if in revenge for the torments he inflicted on his saintly daughter."[30]

Legend says that the name of his wife was the same as that of his daughter's, Sandukht. Sanatruk sacrificed his daughter's life because she refused to give up her Christian faith. Sanatruk's wife, Queen Sandukht, then left her husband. She had twelve children—six sons and six daughters, and when she was dying, she said: "It is better to be the wife of a simple countryman than that of a king who murdered his daughter."

SIRUNIK

The son of the Parthian king Bakur II, Ashkhadar or Shidar, ascended the Armenian throne with the consent of Roman Emperor Trojan (Traianus) and reigned from AD 110 to 113. According to legend, his wife's name was Sirunik. She adored her husband and prompted the court chronicler to write the following statement: "Every queen must keep her dignity and not talk to her maids-of-honor about the passions of her husband."

NAZENIK

Partamasir, another son of the Parthian king, Bakur II Arshakuni, reigned in Armenia from AD 113 to 114. His wife's name was Nazenik. After learning about the death of her husband, who became the victim of a conspiracy, Nazenik changed into peasant's clothing and hid in a village.

"It is better to be a peasant than a queen in captivity and be paraded by Emperor Trajan on the field of Mars," explained Queen Nazenik.

VAGHARSHUHI

Armenian King Vagharsh Arshakuni, son of King Sanatruk, reigned from AD 116 to 144. There is no documentary information available about his wife. However, a tale says that her name was Vagharshuhi.

Queen Vagharshuhi was a modest and wise woman. She suggested that her husband issue an edict that all men older than twenty-four who did not serve in the royal army should pay a special tax toward supporting the army.

"Obviously, this affects only aristocratic families?" asked the king.

"Of course, my king. The peasants are obliged to produce food, but have to be exempted from military taxes."

We don't know if the king issued that edict or not.

SILVA

Armenian King Sohemos reigned from AD 144 to 161 and from AD 164 to 186. According to an old tale, the wife of Sohemos was Roman by origin and shared the name of the Greek goddess of forests and valleys, Silva.

This queen lived in Armenia for many years, but did not learn the Armenian language. When Armenians forcibly drove King Sohemos away from Armenia, they said:

"Maybe we would tolerate your reign for a little longer if your wife knew at least a little Armenian like you."

MAZETA

From AD 161 to 163, Armenian King Bakur Arshakuni reigned. We believe the name of his wife was Mazeta.

When the Romans invaded Artashat and overthrew King Bakur in 163, his wife hid with a maid of honor in the basement of the palace, and after a few days, escaped to Parthia.

ARSHAMUHI

Armenian King Vagharsh II Arshakuni reigned from AD 186 to 198. According to a legend, his wife had the name Arshamuhi. In those times there was a tradition to keep wet-nurses in the court for the infants of the queen. The queens never nursed to keep their beauty and be free from the troubles of nursing. Queen Arshamuhi was a rare exception and nursed her own children.

Also, according to a legend that has reached us, she said, "The queen is a flag of her kingdom's dignity and must soar to inaccessible heights. She must be drawn as a bow all her life. Even her enormous means must be reasonably reduced. She must unriddle every smile and penetrate to the depths of an individual."

Queen Arshamuhi was indeed a wise person.

KHOSROVANUYSH

King of Armenia Khosrov I, the Great, also called Khosrov the Brave, succeeded his father, Vagharsh II Arshakuni, and reigned from AD 211 to 259. Most probably, the name of his wife was Khosrovanuysh.

Khosrov and Khosrovanuysh ruled in those difficult times when the Parthian Arshakuni dynasty was challenged in a life-or-death struggle with the Persian Sasanian dynasty. The Sasanians defeated the Parthians; and after the downfall of the powerful Parthian kingdom and the Arshakuni dynasty, Sasanian King Artashir ascended the Parthian throne. They turned Arshakuni Armenia into a battlefield.

Long-term warfare broke out between Armenia and Persia.

The Sasanians could not reconcile themselves to the rule in Armenia of the kinsmen of their Parthian rivals. The Armenian Arshakunis, in turn, tried to overthrow the Sasanians and return Parthia to their Arshakuni relatives. Many times, Armenian King Khosrov I Arshakuni defeated Artashir Sasanian, but he could not crush the Persian military force completely.

Shapuh I Sasanian succeeded Artashir Sasanian. Khosrov I Arshakuni successfully battled against King Shapuh as well. At that same time, a prince from the Surenian dynasty of Parthia, Anak Pahlavuni, father of the future Gregory the Illuminator, entered a treacherous plot with the Sasanians against the Armenian king. In return for his service, Anak was promised the kingdom of Kushana. Anak came to Armenia along with his entire clan, pretending to be escaping from the oppression of the Persian king. King Khosrov received Prince Anak and his wife Vogohe (or Voguhi) with great honor in his summer residence in the town of Khaghkhagh. The Armenian king settled Prince Anak and his clan in the capital city of Vagharshapat.

Here Voguhi gave birth to their first son, who received the name of the founder of their dynasty, Suren. They placed the newborn under the care of a Christian woman named Sofia.

For seven years, Prince Anak lived in Armenia and enjoyed the hospitality of Khosrov's court. However, Anak never forgot his promise to King Shapuh and waited for an opportunity to keep it.

One day, when Khosrov went hunting, Anak and his brother attacked the Armenian king with their swords and mortally wounded him. They rode away in the direction of Artashat.

Khosrov's bodyguards pursued the killers and encircled them on the Taperian Bridge in Artashat. Seeing no way to escape, Anak and his brother threw themselves into the whirlpools of the Eraskh River and drowned.

In agony, Khosrov ordered all the relatives of Anak murdered. Only little Suren escaped the slaughter, was taken away to Caesarea, and christened there as Gregory. Later, Gregory, a man of Parthian origin and the son of Khosrov's murderer, Anak, became the great preacher of Christianity. He learned the Armenian language, baptized Armenians in the Aratsan (Euphrates) River, and converted Armenia to the Christian faith. He became known as Gregory the Illuminator.

After the death of Khosrov, Shapuh I Sasanian invaded Armenia and subjugated the country. Persians killed the entire royal family, among them Khosrov's wife, Queen Khosrovanuysh. Only two members of the royal family escaped the slaughter—Prince Trdat, Khosrov's son, and Princess Khosrovidukht, his daughter. Artavazd Mandakuni took Trdat to Rome, and Prince Ota Amatuni— along with Princess Khosrovidukht and the royal treasures—escaped to the fortress of Ani. Later, the orphaned Gregory and Trat collaborated to establish the Christian religion in Armenia.

History does not tell us the number of royal children Armenian Queen Khosrovanush had, beside Trdat and Khosrovidukht.

NUSHIK

King Artavazd V ascended the Armenian throne because of the efforts of Persian King Shapuh and reigned from AD 252 to 273. The ancient chroniclers wrote nothing about his queen. A tale says that her name was Nushik. She was an excellent horse-rider and became a winner in competitions with men many times.

SASANDUKHT

Vormizd (Hormizd)-Artashir, son of the Sasanian Persian King Shapuh I, was named king of Armenia from AD 261 to 273. Legend says that his wife Sasandukht, who was Persian by origin, had to leave Armenia for her homeland with her husband, against her will.

She said to people close to her: "Armenians did not like my husband, but they treated me with respect. Generally, women in Armenia enjoy greater respect and honor than in any other county in this world. If I had a choice, I would have remained in Armenia, I would have married an Armenian prince, and I would have been happy. It wasn't the Armenian people who drove me out of the country, but my royal crown."

NERSEHANUYSH

Another son of the Persian King Shapuh I, Nerseh, succeeded his brother Hormizd- Artashir and was named king in Armenia from AD 273 to 287. Legend says that the name of his wife was Nersehanuysh.

This Persian woman, who had been an Armenian queen for fourteen years, was a very clever woman. After her husband was overthrown, she returned to Persia.

Her mother asked her: "What did Armenia give you, my daughter?"

"Nothing," answered Nersehanuysh, "because Armenia did not want me as her queen. No woman would like to be a queen and enter a mousetrap, where all the splendor, luxury, happiness, wealth, and glory is just shining tinsel. But no woman can become a queen by her own will. Queens are only the wives of their ruling husbands. I was the queen of Armenia only in name, and the Armenians and their country has always been alien to me. I neither gave anything to Armenia, nor received anything from Armenia."

ASHKHEN

King Trdat III the Great, son of Armenian King Khosrov I Arshakuni, reigned from AD 287 to 330. He married Ashkhen, the daughter of the Alan King Ashkhadar. In AD301. While Ashkhen was queen, Christianity was declared the state religion of Armenia.

Historian Movses Khorenatsi wrote, "Returning to Armenia, Trat sent Knight Smbat, the father of Bagarat, to bring the daughter of Ashkhadar, Ashkhen, as a bride. She was as tall as Trdat himself. He ordered her to be named Arshakuni and placed the crown on her head. They gave birth to a son Khosrov, whose height was not comparable to the height of his parents."[31]

Ashkhen was the first Christian Armenian queen, and she promoted the dissemination of the Christian faith throughout the nation.

Ancient chronicler Agatangeghos affirms that Ashkhen took part in the burial of the remains of the Hripsimé virgins. He also writes about the baptism of the Armenian queen:

"Saint Gregory gathered the people and the king himself, his wife Ashkhen, their daughter Khosrovidukht, and all the high-ranking men of the court and army, and took them to the banks of the Euphrates River and baptized all of them 'in name of the Father and Son and Holy Spirit.'[32] "[33]

At the end of her life Ashkhen, following her husband, retreated to Garni fortress, where she lived a monastic life until her last day.[32,33]

CHAKHRUHI

Khosrov II Arshakuni succeeded his father, Trdat the Great, and ruled as king of Armenia from AD 330 to 338. He received the nickname "Kotak" for his short height.

When it was the time for Kotak to get married, the tallest girls from the different parts of Armenia gathered.

Legend says that the tallest of them, by the name of Chakhruhi, from the town of Daruynk, became the wife of Kotak. Later, the joke at the court was that after his marriage, Kotak grew by one inch.

BAMBISH

The Armenian king Tiran succeeded his father, Khosrov II Kotak, and reigned from AD 338 to 350. We don't know the name of Tiran's wife, and we will call her Bambish.

Bambish gave birth to the most rebellious king in the Arshakuni dynasty, Arshak II. After being dethroned (and blinded by the Persian king Shapuhed), Tiran with his wife moved to the village of Kuash (present Kosh) in the province of Aragatson, where they spent their last years. Following the death of her husband, Bambish visited Tiran's grave every day, and before her death said that Tiran had been waiting for her.

"Her soul has hurried to Tiran," said her maid of honor to the gathered people.

PARANDZEM

Arshak II Arshakuni, king of Armenia, succeeded his father Tiran and reigned from AD 350 to 368. His wife, Queen Parandzem, was the aunt of the well-known Prince Vasak Syuni. Arshak was also married to the Greek princess Olympia. Parandzem had a bright individuality.

Armenian chroniclers have both praise and criticism for this queen. Movses Khorenatsi adduced the following story regarding Parandzem's first husband, Gnel, son of King Arshak's slain brother, Trdat.

"Now Gnel came to the town of Kuash at the foot of the mountain called Aragats to his blinded grandfather Tiran, for he was still alive. Tiran lamented bitterly over his son Trat, Gnel's father, holding himself responsible for his murder. Therefore, he gave all his possessions to Gnel, along with his holdings of villages and estates, ordering him to live in that same town of Kuash. Then Gnel took a certain Parandzem of the Syuni family as his wife. He celebrated the wedding royally, giving presents to all the princes."

"They were pleased and friendly toward him and gave him their children. These he accepted and grandly equipped them with arms and finery, so they loved him all the more. Here Tirit, (Gel's cousin, son of King Arshak's brother, Artashesed) found a pretext for calumny. Approaching the king with his friend Vardan, the king's arms-bearer who was of the Mamikonian family, they said, 'Don't you know that Gnel is plotting to kill you and seize the throne? Behold, see the proof of the matter, O King. Gnel has taken up residence in Ayrarat in your royal lands, and the affection of all the princes is on his side. For the emperors have contrived this by giving him the honor of the consulate and much treasure with which he has bribed the princes. Vardan swore by the king's sun, saying, 'With my own ears I have heard Gnel saying, "I shall not abandon the avenging of my father's death on my uncle on whose account it occurred." '

"King Arshak believed these stories. In those times, there was a tradition that only the king and his son/heir had the right to settle in Ayrarat. The other members of the Arshakuni family could live in the provinces of Hashtiank, Aghiovit, and Arberani at the expense of the royal count. King Arshak thus sent Vardan to tell Gnel that he had to choose between death or leaving the province of Ararat and sending back the sons of the princes. Gnel obeyed the king's command and moved to the provinces of Aghiovit and Arberan."

Then Moves Khorenatsi describes how King Arshak ordered his sword bearer,

Vardan, to kill Gnel during a hunting trip. Then Gnel was buried in Zarishat, while the king and the princes pretended to mourn him.

Continuing the story, the ancient historian writes, "Arshak showed no repentance or contrition but shamelessly rifled the treasures and inheritance of the dead man and even married his wife Parandzem. From her was born a son, who was called Pap.

"This Parandzem worked an unheard of and unimaginable crime worthy of inspiring horror in those who heard of it. Through an unworthy priest, falsely so named, she mixed mortal poison in the remedy of life and gave it to Olympia, Arshak's first wife, depriving her of life through envy for her queenly rank."[34] The Persian king Shapuh, after drawing Arshak into a trap and capturing him, forced him to invite Parandzem to the Persian court, with the purpose of capturing her too.

But as Moves Khorenatsi writes: "Queen Parandzem did not obey her husband's summons, but with the treasures took refuge in the castle of Artagerk and warned her son Pap, hoping to escape from Shapuh's hands. But Shapuh, incensed at them, bound Arshak's feet in iron chains and had him taken to the land of Khuzastan, to the fortress called Anush. Gathering many troops under Mehruzhan Artsruni and Vahan Mamikonian, apostates of Christ, he attacked Armenia. They came and took the castle of Artagerk. And although they could not take it because of its impenetrable defenses, yet because God's anger was on Arshak, the garrison of the fortress refused to wait for news of Pap and surrendered willingly, without compulsion. Taking them captive with the treasures and Queen Parandzem, they brought them to Assyria. And there they massacred them by impaling them on wagon poles."[35]

Historian Pavstos Buzand, who also devoted many pages to Parandzem, gives a slightly different account of these events. According to Pavstos: "In those times Andovk, one prince of province of Siunik, had a beautiful daughter named Parandzem who was renowned for her beauty and her modesty, and the young nephew of the king, Gnel, took her as his wife. The fame of the maiden's loveliness spread, and the renown of her beauty grew, increased, and resounded. Another cousin of Gnel, named Tirit, quivered with desire toward his cousin's wife because of this fame, and he sought some secret way whereby he might see her. Once he had succeeded in seeing the one whom he desired, he sought a means of destroying the woman's husband so that he might perhaps be able to carry her off afterward."

Like Khorenatsi, Pavstos Buzand maintains that Tirit convinced King Arshak that Gnel plotted against him to ascend the throne, and thus provoked his assassination.

Pavstos continues: "When [Parandzem] saw her husband seized and bound, she ran in haste . . . to the camp, as they were offering morning prayers and the great chief-bishop Nerses was also present."

Appealing to the great Archbishop Nerses, who was conducting the divine service, she cried out: "Hurry, go! They are unjustly killing my husband, who has done no harm or wrong!"

Nerses halted the service and rushed to the king's room. When the king saw the great archbishop entering, he guessed he had come to plead for the life of Gnel, and Arshak pretended to be asleep, so he should not appear to hear the words.

Pavstos Buzand colorfully described the tragic sight: "They took the young Gnel near the royal horse wall and they beheaded him on a hill in the mountains at the place called Lin near the fence enclosing the hunting ground opposite the royal feasting hall, at the myrtle springs in front of the home camp. Then the king ordered everyone, without exception, to mourn the death of the young prince, Gnel Arshakuni.

"And the king himself went among the mourners and sat weeping over his nephew, whom he himself had killed," Pavstos Buzand continues. "As for Parandzem, the wife of the slain, rending her garments and loosening her hair, she lamented with bosom bared among the mourners. She wailed aloud and made all weep by the mournful tears of her grievous lament. But when King Arshak saw the wife of the murdered man among the wailers, he was stricken with passion, and desired to take her as his wife."

King Arshak gave orders to kill Tirit, who was in love with Parandzem, and married the widowed beauty. But, according to Pavstos Buzand, Parandzem hated the king as much as he loved her, and complained, "His body is hairy and his skin is dark."

Later, Parandzem became very jealous of Arshak's other wife, Olympia, and poisoned her with the help of a lay brother by the name of Mriyunik. King Shapuh executed Queen Parandzem in a most barbarous way.

"He ordered a device for debauchery erected in the public square and had the woman thrown onto it . . . And in this fashion, they killed Parandzem the queen."[36]

Writing about the tragic life of Parandzem, Vardan Hatsuni notes that this woman was a well-known figure of the century, mostly because of her beauty and modesty, her title, her matrimonial adventures, her revengefulness, courage, and tragic death. [35] The freedom-loving soul of Parandzem has remained in many generations of Armenian women and reached our times. In 1990, during the war for the liberation of Artsakh, a female military unit called "Parandzem" was distinguished by its unusual courage in victorious battles.[36]

OLYMPIA

The name of the other wife of King Arshak I was Olympia, who was Hellenic by origin. Historian Pavstos Buzand writes: "King Arshak sent a messenger to the land of the Greeks and brought from there a wife of the race of the imperial house, whose name was Olompi [Olympia]. And he loved her greatly and thus aroused the jealousy of his first wife. Parandzem nourished a great jealousy and resentment against Olympia, and she sought to kill her."

The historian continues by writing that Olympia "was most careful of herself, especially in food and drink, for she ate [only] food prepared by her maidservants and wine presented by them. And so, when no way could be found to infect her with a deadly poison, the iniquitous Parandzem then persuaded a certain priest from the royal court named Mrjyunik from a locality in Arshamunik, from the province of the district of Taron, who was there at the time.

"And he performed an unworthy, unprecedented, unatonable, evilly sinful and unforgettable deed [worthy of eternal] torments—[a deed that was] unworthy, never seen, and unheard of: that is, to mix into the draught of life the draught of death. mortal poison was mixed into the holy and divine Body of the Lord, into the bread of the Eucharist, and in the church the priest named Mrjyunik gave [this] death-dealing thing to Queen Olympia and so killed her."[37,38]

Movses Khorenatsi wrote, in a similar story differing in some details, that it was Archbishop Nerses who Arshak sent to meet the Roman Emperor Theodosius, following the Armenian defeat in battle. Nerses negotiated a peace with the emperor and he "brought as a wife for Arshak a maiden called Olympias from the imperial family." Khorenatsi affirms the story that Parandzem plotted with Mrjyunik to poison Olympia by mixing poison in the communion bread and giving it to Olympia during the divine service.[39,40]

Acharian writes that Queen Olympia was from the Greek emperor's family, daughter of the emperor's chief guard, Ablabios, and formerly betrothed to Constans, the emperor's deceased brother. According to the historian Ammianus, Arshak married Olympia in AD 360. [41] Olympia was poisoned and died in AD 362; hence, she was queen of Armenia for only two to three years.

ZARMANDUKHT

King Pap Arshakuni succeeded his father, Arshak II, and reigned from AD 370 to 374.

According to Pavstos Buzand, the name of his wife was Zarmandukht. After the death of King Pap, the military leader of Armenia, Manuel Mamikonian, proclaimed Zarmandukht the queen of Armenia and the regent for her under-aged princes.

"The king of Persia also sent a crown, a robe of honor, and the royal standard to Queen Zarmandukht, as well as crowns for her two young sons, Arshak and Vagharshak."[42]

Vardan Hatsuni writes that "judging by her name, the wife of King Pap, Zarmandukht, was an Armenian woman from Byzantium."[43]

ROMELA

Succeeding his uncle (King Pap), King Varazdat Arshakuni reigned from AD 374 to 378. King Varazdat married before he ascended the throne at the time when he became famous in Rome as a winner in the Olympic games (in boxing).

Legend says that the daughter of a senator by the name of Romela saw one of Varazdat's matches, fell in love with him, and confessed her feelings to him.

Varazdat liked the beautiful Roman girl and brought her to Armenia. Probably, after Varazdat's down-fall, she left Armenia and returned to Rome.

VARDANDUKHT

King Arshak III Arshakuni was the son of King Pap and reigned from AD 378 to 390. His wife's name was Vardandukht. Pavstos Buzand writes: "The military leader Manuel gave his daughter Vardandukht in marriage to the young Arshak Arshakuni and thus made him his son-in-law."[44] This is the only documentary evidence about this queen.

It is interesting to note that only a few daughters from the famous Mamikonian dynasty became queens. Probably the Armenian Arshakunis hesitated to establish a close family relationship with the famous dynasty, fearing that the throne might pass to the Mamikonians. This is an assumption only, and nothing more.

SMBATUHI

Vagharshak, the younger son of King Pap, reigned with his elder brother Arshak III from AD 378 to 390. About King Vagharshak, Pavstos Buzand writes that the military leader Manuel Mamikonian arranged his marriage, "giving him the daughter of the Bagratuni cavalry commander from the district of Sper, who had been the royal consort from the very origin of the Arshakuni royal clan."[45]

Hence, we can name her Smbatuhi after the most prominent name of the Bagratuni dynasty, Smbat.

We know nothing more about the life of this Armenian queen.

ZRVANDUKHT

The Persian King Shapuh III Sasanian appointed the young Khosrov III Arshakuni as Armenian king, at the request of some of the Armenian princes, and married him to his sister, Zrvandukht. Khosrov III reigned from AD 385 to 388 and in AD 415.

Pavstos Buzand wrote that King Shapuh III designated as king of Armenia from the Arshakuni royal dynasty "a youth named Khosrov, placed the crown on his head, and gave him his [own] sister Zrvandukht as a wife."[45]

Nothing more is reported about this Armenian queen of Persian origin.

GEGHANUYSH

King Vramshapuh succeeded his brother, Khosrov III Arshakuni, and reigned from AD 389 to 414. An ancient legend says that the name of Vramshapuh's wife was Geghanuysh.

Together with her husband, she promoted the creation of the Armenian alphabet by Mesrop Mashtots and Sahak Partev.

On her tombstone, which has not been preserved, it was written "Queen Geghanuysh" in Armenian letters. This was the first tombstone with Armenian letters carved on it.

SHAPUHDUKHT

Shapuh the Persian was appointed to the Armenian throne and reigned from AD 416 to 419. He was the son and heir of the Sasanian King Hakert I. A tale says that the name of King Shapuh's wife was Shapuhdukht. She became a queen at the end of his reign and ruled for only four days.

On the night of the fourth day, she was forcibly seated in a carriage and sent back to Persia. On the way, an Armenian military unit stopped her carriage. The men took away only her royal crown and said, "You don't need this any longer."

KNKUSH

Artashes II Arshakuni (who is called Artashir by Movses Khorenatsi) was the son of Vramshapuh Arshakuni and the last king of the Arshakuni dynasty. He reigned from AD 422 to 428. The name of his wife has not reached us, but a legend says that it was Knkush. This beautiful Armenian woman loved her husband with an unrequited love.

She deeply suffered from his infidelity, but she held high her royal dignity. And when she learned about the downfall of her husband, she threw herself down from a high rock and perished. [46]

KINGDOMS OF OSRONE AND ARTSAHK

HAYRANUYSH

The Armenian king of Osroene, Abgar VII, reigned from AD 109 to 116. We don't know the name of his wife, and we will call this Armenian queen Hayranuysh.

A tale says that King Abgar's wife did not like covered carriages and believed that one was most likely to become the victim of a plot in such a conveyance. We know nothing else about Hayranuysh.

HOVADUKHT

Abgar VIII, the Armenian king of Osroene, reigned from AD 116 to 178. According to a tale, his wife's name was Hovadukht. This Armenian queen had a very keen ear. She could even hear whispering in an adjacent room.

The court people were astonished that she always knew about every conversation at court. However, we don't know whether she ever took advantage of her unusual capability.

SOPIA

The Armenian king of Osroene, Abgar IX, reigned from AD 179 to 214. If we believe the legend, his wife named Sopia [Sophia] was a Christian.

She kept her faith a secret from her husband and others. Sopia prayed and worshiped quietly in her mind; and although the king and queen lived together for many years, the king never learned about his wife's Christian faith.

HURAMA

The king of Artsakh and Utik, Vaché, reigned in the fifth century. He married the daughter of the Sasanian King Hakert II's sister. In my unpublished historical novel *Vachagan*, I called her Hurama, and that fictional name I will keep here.

Evidently, she was a queen in Artsakh for only a short time, and she returned to Tizbon when her husband became a hermit and withdrew to the village of Avetaranots.

SHUSHANIK

Vachagan III Barepasht ("the Pious") reigned in Artsakh and Utik from 450 to 510 AD. The name of Vachagan's wife was Shushanik. Movses Kaghankatvatsi writes:

"The queen of Aghvank, Shushanik, who was a very religious and kind-hearted woman, ordered her big marquee installed over the red room of saints like a church, since that place was often visited by the members of the royal court, by the king, and many others."

The same historian reports that Queen Shushanik had a son by the name of Pandalion and a daughter named Khnchik.[47] In the republic of Mountainous Karabagh, there is a river by the name of Shushana, which springs from the slopes of Mount Kirs.

According to legend, this river is called by the name of Queen Shushanik.

The proper name Shushan (or Shushanik) originated from the name of the flower Shushan ("lily"), but Shushan or Susan had been adopted from the ancient Pahlavenian language and means "clean, unblemished." Probably there was a tradition in the royal court of calling women who became queen by that name.

About Queen Shushanik, we may add the following. In Artsakh and Utik, there was a custom of referring to the royal consort as a "World-woman" (ashkharhatikin), which was the synonym for the word "queen" in those provinces.

MEDIEVAL KINGDOMS

GRIGORYANUSH

The Armenian king of Arevelkits Koghmants (Eastern Country), Hamam Areveltsi, reigned in the second part of ninth century (the year 894 has been mentioned in historical sources). His kingdom included the entire territory of Vachagan Barepasht's kingdom, including the provinces of Artsakh, Utik, and Kambejan. King Hamam Areveltsi and his wife are buried in the village of Avetaranots in Artsakh.

More than one thousand years have passed since King Hamam and Queen Grigoryanuysh were buried in the cemetery of the village of Avetaranots. On the tombstone of the queen, only a woman's profile is carved. On the tombstone of King Hamam, the inscription had been obliterated, and in 1241 a certain "Ter Masan" erected a new tombstone.[48]

The name of Queen Grigoranush has been passed from generation to generation, but we don't know who her father Grigor was—perhaps a prince or a commander?

In the memories of local people, a tale has survived, according to which Queen Grigoryanuysh once a year presented a silver coin to each villager. People did not forget the generosity of this queen.

KATRANIDÉ

The founder of the Bagratuni royal family, King Ashot I the Great, reigned from 885 to 890. The name of Ashot Bagratuni's wife was Katranidé.[49] In an inscription from Garni, dated 879, Ashot's wife Katranidé is described as an Armenian queen.[50]

She gave birth to the princes Smbat and Abas.

King Ashot gave one of their daughters [Sopi, or Sophia] in marriage to Prince Derenik [Artsruni] of Vaspurakan, and the other daughter, Mariam, was given as a wife to Vasak Gabur from the Syuni family, who reigned at the time as prince of Gegharkunik Province.

Katranidé was a wise woman who helped her husband in governing the kingdom.

ASHOTDUKHT

King Smbat I Bagratuni succeeded his father Ashot I and reigned from 890 to 914. The name of his wife was Ashotdukht. Historians say almost nothing about this queen. A legend suggests that this courageous woman participated in her husband's campaigns. Once she straddled a fast horse, speeded ahead with her hair loose and flying, and caused a panic among the enemy forces. They thought she was a goddess from the heavens who had come to punish them, and they fled from the battlefield.

Yes, Armenians did have a queen like Ashotdukht!

SAHAKANUYSH

King Ashot II Erkat ("Iron"), son of Smbat Bagratuni, reigned from 914 to 929. He was married to the daughter of Sahak Sevada, the prince of Gargman province. The Armenian writer Muratsan, in his historical novel Gevorg Marzpetuni, named Ashot Erkat's wife Sahakanuysh. In those times, daughters rarely had names and mostly were referred to by the names of their fathers.

Ashot II Erkat and Sahak Sevada always had a strained relationship. It is clear that Queen Sahakanuysh felt this tension and could not be indifferent. In the beginning, Sahak Sevada helped his son-in-law, King Ashot Erkat, to consolidate his power, but later Sevada rebelled against him twice. Ashot Erkat suppressed the revolts, captured his father-in-law in 923, and blinded him. Ashot II Erkat and Sahakanush had no children.

MARIAM

Abas, the younger son of Smbat I Bagratuni, succeeded his older brother Ashot II Erkat and reigned from 929 to 953. The name of King Abas Bagratuni's wife has not reached us. Here we call her Mariam.

That Armenian queen undoubtedly strongly supported her courageous husband, who was a great builder. The royal couple together supported the construction of the Apostolic church in the city of Kars, which remains standing to this day. A legend says that Queen Mariam was buried near that church.

KHOSROVANUYSH

King Ashot III Voghormats ("the Merciful") succeeded his father, Abas Bagratuni, and reigned from 953 to 977. His wife was Khosrovanuysh. In 966, this royal couple established the monastery of Sanahin. In 976, they founded the monastery of Haghpat and donated generous gifts. They also established a pilgrimage site on Lake Sevan.

Queen Khosrovanuysh was a great philanthropist in medieval Armenia. We know also that her daughter Hripsimé became a nun. Khosrovanuysh died in 980.[51]

KATRANIDÉ

Armenian King Smbat Bagratuni, known as Tiezerakal ("Master of the Universe"), reigned from 958 jointly with his father, Ashot III Voghormats, and alone from 977 to 989. Mkhitar Anetsi reports that the name of Smbat's wife was Katranidé and that the two sponsored the construction of the foundation for a large cathedral in Ani.

It is possible that there is some confusion here, because it is known that the wife of Gagik I Bagratuni, the brother of Smbat and future king, also had the same name.

King Smbat greatly contributed to the construction of Ani. For that reason, the walls of the fortress of Ani were called by his name, Smbatashen. It is probable that Queen Katranidé was also a benefactor. But nothing is known about the good works of this queen.

KATRANIDÉ

King Gagik, I succeeded his brother, Smbat Bagratuni, and reigned from 989 to 1020. Queen Katranidé, his wife, was the daughter of King Vasak I of Syunik. The valley of the river Oghju in the province of Syunik gave two remarkable women to the world, Queens Parandzem and Katranidé.

Stepanos Orbelian writes: "King Gagik became the son-in-law of King Vasak, whose daughter became Queen Katranidé."[52]

In the city of Ani, the mother cathedral, whose foundations were laid by King Smbat II in 989, was completed in 1001 during the time of King Gagik I with the patronage of his wife, Katranidé. The capital city of Ani flourished, complete with beautiful architectural monuments, mainly from the end of the tenth century and into the first two decades of the eleventh century, thanks to three notable Armenian personalities: architect Trat, King Gagik I Bagratuni, and Queen Katranidé.

Writing about Queen Katranide's role in the building and embellishing of the Ani cathedral, historian Stepanos Asoghik (Taronetsi) writes: "The pious queen . . . completed the building of the church founded by Smbat, a magnificent edifice with lofty vaults and a sanctuary surmounted by a heaven-like cupola. And she adorned it with tapestries embroidered with purple flowers woven with gold and painted in various colors, and with vessels of silver and gold through whose resplendent brilliance the holy cathedral in the city of Ani shone forth like the heavenly vault."[53]

If fortune ever gives the Armenian people an opportunity to rebuild Ani, it would be necessary to erect there a statue of Queen Katranidé and to carve the following on the pedestal: "The devout and pious Armenian Queen Katranidé did everything possible to adorn Ani with magnificent buildings and constructions, donating all of her wealth, including her dowry, for that purpose." They buried Gagik I and Katranidé side by side in the crypt near Ani cathedral, built by the order of Katranidé.

During the archeological excavations in Ani at the beginning of the twentieth century, when Nicholas Marr dug out the skeleton of Queen Katranidé, they found her legs crossed like those of Jesus Christ on the cross. This is a singular burial in the Christian world, which has not occurred before, or since, her time.

Apparently, the queen wanted to be buried in that manner in order to confirm, even after death, her devotion to the Christian faith. Vardan Hatsuni has written: "N. Marr, in removing her skeleton from the cemetery in Ani, with her two feet crossed, one over the other, wished but was unable to find the significance. It is a unique thing, and not known in our ancient burial traditions. Why not suppose that the great queen arranged to accomplish in death what she could not in life, that is to nail her feet together in the manner of the crucified Savior, something that no other Christian ever thought of doing?"[54]

Devout Queen Katranidé, with her magnificent buildings, in a certain way made Armenia a little more Armenian. She knew that churches and monuments built on the Armenian land are in perfect harmony with the Armenian mountainous terrain, and they have Christianized the Armenian environment. Armenian church buildings have become an integral part of the Armenian landscape.

SHUSHAN

King Hovhannes Smbat Bagratuni was the older son of Gagik I and reigned with his brother Ashot IV from 1020 to 1041. Hovhannes Smbat Bagratuni's wife was the daughter of a certain Abas.

According to Acharian, an inscription dated 1038, discovered in the province of Shirak, recorded this information.

Acharian writes also that the name of this woman was Shushan. In the museum of the Holy See of Etchmiadzin, there is a silver cross with her name engraved on it.[55]

This Armenian queen had no children, and most probably King Hovhannes Smbat divorced her before 1032.

FLORA

In 1032, King Hovhannes Smbat Bagratuni married the daughter of the brother of the Byzantine emperor Romanus III (Argyropolus). This woman, whom we call Flora from the name of the Greek goddess of flowers, gave birth to a son who died at a very young age. This Armenian queen of Greek origin soon left Armenia and returned to Byzantium.

TAGUHI

King Ashot IV Bagratuni reigned from 1020 to 1041. We don't know the name of his wife, but here we will call her Taguhi. King Ashot IV and Taguhi had one son, named after his grandfather Gagik, and reigned from 1042 to 1045. Gagik was the last representative of the Bagratuni royal family to become king.

GRIGORADUKHT

The king of Vaspurakan, Gagik Artsruni, or Gagik-Khachik Artsruni, reigned from 908 to 943. The historian Tovma Artsruni claims that Gagik Artsruni was married to the daughter of the lord of Archuchk fortress, Prince Grigor Abuhamza. Tovma does not mention her name, which most probably was Grigoradukht, after her father.

Once the father-in-law rebelled against his son-in-law. However, Gagik Artsruni suppressed the revolt, seized the fortress of Archuchk, and spared his father-in- law's life.

This event had a profound effect upon the relations between King Gagik Artsruni and Grigoradukht, however. Gagik divorced the queen and later remarried.

MLKÉ

After divorcing his first wife, King Gagik Artsruni of Vaspurakan married a woman by the name of Mlké. They also knew her as Tamar. Acharian writes that Tamar in Hebrew means "palm tree" and notes that the queen was from a royal family. The second wife of King Gagik I Artsruni, Queen Mlké (Tamar), was the daughter of Prince Shapuh, the brother of King Smbat I.[56]

Queen Mlké took part together with her husband in the construction of churches and temples in Armenia. The most beautiful and magnificent Armenian Church of the Holy Cross on the island of Akhtamar was built in 915–921 by order of King Gagik Artsruni and Queen Mlké. The architect of this church was the famous Manuel.

The church of Akhtamar occupies the first place in the list of Armenian architectural wonders. On the west front of the church is carved a bas-relief of King Gagik Artsruni holding a model of the church in his hands. Pictures of the king's mother, Princess Sopi, and the king's wife, Queen Mlké, are also carved near the walls of the church.

The name of Mlké is also connected with an Armenian manuscript, T*he Gospel of Queen Mlké*, which was written in Vaspurakan in 862. Later, it was stolen from the monastery of Varag, but in 922, Queen Mlké found it and returned to the monastery.

Now that well-preserved ancient Armenian manuscript is kept in the book depository of the Mkhitarist Order in Venice (Manuscript N 1144186).

GURGENDUKHT

The king of Vaspurakan Derenik Artsruni, or Ashot Derenik Artsruni, reigned from 943 to 958. The chronicler of the Artsruni family, Tovma Artsruni, wrote nothing about the wife of this king.

A Vaspurakan tale says that the name of this queen was Gurgendukht. She tried to emulate Queen Mlké in charitable work, but her husband impeded all her attempts at charity and, according to the tale, this was the reason for her premature death.

KATA

King of Vaspurakan Abusahl-Hamazasp Artsruni reigned from 958 to 968. His wife's name was Kata. Her sons Gurgen-Khachik, Ashot-Sahak, and Senekerim-Hovannes became kings of Vaspurakan. We know nothing else about Queen Kata.

DERENIKUHI

Ashot-Sahak Artsruni, the king of Vaspurakan, reigned from 977 to 990. An old tale in Vaspurakan says that the wife of this king was called by the name of her father, Prince Derenik. We know nothing about her father. The same tale says Derenikuhi was an extraordinary swimmer and could swim in Lake Van for many hours without becoming tired.

GAYANÉ

Gurgen Khachik Artsruni, the king of Vaspurakan, reigned in the province of Andzevatsik from 977 to 1003. The name of his wife has not been recorded in any original source, but a tale says that her name was Gayané. She was the most beautiful woman in all Vaspurakan, and she was very self-enamored. She insisted her husband carve the following apothegm on a stone:

"All the beauties kept away from the queen of Vaspurakan Gayané, so they do not look ugly."

It is said that the young women of Andzevatsik broke that stone, and Gayané ordered a new one carved. This one was again broken. We don't know how many times this process was repeated, and the stone has not survived the passing years.

KHUSHUSH

Senekerim-Hovhannes Artsruni, the king of Vaspurakan, reigned from 968 to 1025. He married Khushush, the daughter of King Gagik I.

According to Acharian, the origin of this woman's name is unknown. Queen Khushush ordered the church of Saint Sophia built in the monastery of the Holy Sign of Varag in 981.

At first, King Senekerim-Hovannes reigned in his native land of Vaspurakan. Pressed by his enemies, "he ceded his native Vaspurakan to the impostor Vasil and took in return for that land in the city of Sebastia with its neighboring areas."[57]

Thus, in 1021, victims of the insidious politics of Byzantium, Senekerim-Hovhannes Artsruni and Queen Khushush lost their native Vaspurakan (including eight towns, seventy-two fortresses, and four thousand villages) to the emperor of Byzantium and received in return the province of Sebastia.

"Khushush, it is very difficult for us to leave our native country, but Sebastia is also an Armenian land," said Senekerim-Hovhannes.

Senekerim-Hovanness launched massive construction in Sebastia, but it had been a mistake for the royal couple to leave their native land, and both suffered far from their homeland.

They died in Sebastia, but probably their remains were moved to Vaspurakan for burial. Acharian wrote that the tombs of Khushush and her husband were in the monastery of Varag.[58] There is a tale about Khushush that when her husband asked her why she did not wear jewelry and fine clothes, she answered:

"My husband, you are spending your treasury on the construction of beautiful stone churches, temples, and fortresses, dressing our land with beautiful stone clothes. I completely approve of it. The dresses of the queen will wear out, but the stone monuments will preserve their beauty for ages."

PARISUHI

The founder of the Armenian kingdom of Kars, Mushegh I, reigned from 963 to 984.

He was married to the sister of King Senekerim. Vardan Hatsuni calls her Parisuhi; however, her real name is unknown.[59]

After the death of her husband, Parisuhi renounced her secular lifestyle and founded the convent of Trin in the province of Arsharunik, in the Ayrarat region of Greater Armenia, where she became the abbess.

GORANDUKHT

Abas Bagratuni, the king of Kars, reigned from 984 to 1029.

The name of his wife was Gorandukht. Hatsuni writes that there exists a painting dating from the eleventh century in which the King Gagik, Queen Gorandukht, and their daughter Mariam are portrayed sitting on an ottoman, with the queen in the center and her daughter and the king on her two sides.

We don't know anything else about this queen.

GORANDUKHT

The king of Kars, Gagik Abasian, or Gagik of Kars, who was also a poet, reigned from 1029 to 1065. The son of King Abas, Gagik, married Gorandukht, the sister of the king of Abkhazia and Georgia, Bagrat IV (1027–1072).[60]

This Armenian queen had a very difficult life, but always remained an agreeable companion for her husband. Unable to withstand the invasions of alien hordes, Gagik of Kars ceded his territories to the emperor of Byzantium and received in return the towns of Tsamndav, Laris, Komana, and Amasia (in Cilicia).

Gagik was the last king of the Armenian kingdom of Kars, and Gorandukht was the last Armenian queen of Kars. Historians report nothing else about Queen Gorandukht.

ARUSYAK

The king of Lori, Gurgen (or Kyurike), son of King Ashot III Voghormats and the founder of the Kyurikian kingdom, reigned from 966 to 991. The name of his queen is unknown. We will call her Arusyak. According to Hatsuni, this was one of the most popular names of Ani's Bagratuni family.

A tale holds that this queen loved grapes, which were served on her table all year round. Queen Arusyak gave birth to princes Davit (later known as Davit Anhoghin) and Smbat.

ZORAKRTSEL

Davit Anhoghin ("Lackland" or "Landless"), the Armenian king of Lori, reigned from 996 to 1084. His wife was Zorakrtsel, daughter of the Kakhetian King Kyurike III.[61]

King Davit Anhoghin and Queen Zorakrtsel, a Georgian by origin, had two sons, Kyurike and Gagik, and a daughter, Hranush. We don't have any other documentary information about Queen Zorakrtsel.

HRIPSIMÉ

Kyurike I Bagratuni, the king of Tashir-Dzoraget, reigned from 1048 to 1089. We don't know the name of his wife, but legend says that this faithful and kind-hearted Armenian queen had the name Hripsimé. She gave birth to three sons, Davit, Abas, and Stepanos, and a daughter whose name has not come down to us.

The name of the king's sister Hranush is also mentioned in one source as Queen Hranush. We do not know, however, whose wife she was and why she had the title of queen.

MAMKAN

Abas I, the last king of the Kyurikian royal dynasty, descendants of the Bagratuni family, reigned (together with his brother Davit) in Lori from 1090 to 1113. King Abas I was married to a woman by the name of Mamkan, who later became a churchwoman (gronavoruhi). [62]

No other information about this queen is available.

RUZUKAN

The last Kyurikian King, Davit, reigned (with his brother Abas I) in Lori from 1090 to 1113. His wife, by the name of Ruzukan, like Queen Mamkan, took holy orders and entered a convent.[61] She had a son named Kyurike and a daughter, Ruzukan.

SEDA

Senekerim, or Hovhannes-Senekerim, the Armenian king of Parisos, reigned from 958 to 1003. We will call his wife Seda.[63]

Senekerim's sister was the wife of the king of Kars, Mushegh, and the mother of Abas. We assume her name was Parishi.

Every year she sent a little box full of jewelry to her brother's wife, Seda. As she explained once, she did this so that Seda might love her husband even more.

SHAHANDUKHT

The king of Syunik, Smbat I Sahakian, reigned from 987 to 998. He was married to the daughter of Prince Sevada of Aghvan, Shahandukht.

Stepanos Orbelian writes: "In those days Smbat, the son of Sahak and sovereign of Syunik, died. He was buried in the diocese of Tate. The faithful Queen Shahandukht and her sons Vasak and Sevada donated six thousand drams to the holy church for the soul of the faithful and pious King Smbat. They also donated the village Tegh in Haband province, which had been built by the order of the queen herself."

These events took place in 998.

The historian of Syunik continues that Queen Shahandukht "moved by a divine vision, also built the beautiful monastery of Vaghatn in the place that had been a pilgrimage site since ancient times because Saint Gregory the Illuminator Church stood there once." I believe Saint Gregory himself founded the church.

Father Stepanos and the holy fathers (hermits) later rebuilt it. He cured those bitten by poisonous snakes.

"And for this reason, the pious queen Shahandukht built here a carved stone church in the name of Saint Stepanos in the Armenian year of 449 (1000) and established lodging for many clergy and servants of the monastery. In the courtyard of the church, she built also a chapel made of limestone (tufa), as well as workshops, and storehouses, and a strong wall surrounding the monastery. She established the boundaries of the monastery in Vaghatn and turned over to its possession the large farm of Gomer. Upon her death, she was buried in the courtyard of this same holy place."[64]

KUPGHIDUKHT

Vasak I, the king of Syunik, reigned from 998 to 1040. We don't know the name of his wife and will call her Kupghidukht, which was a popular aristocratic name in medieval Syunik. Queen Kupghidukht did not have a son, but she gave birth to a daughter named Katranidé, the future wife of King Gagik I Bagratuni, the famous queen of the Armenian capital Ani.

Stepanos Orbelian writes: "Then King Vasak died and was buried beside his father Smbat. Because he did not have an heir, the throne passed to Ashot's son Smbat."[64] Ashot was Vasak's and Kupghidukht's son-in-law, and Smbat was their grandson.

SOPI

The king of Syunik, Smbat II Ashotian, reigned from 1040 to 1044. We don't know the name of his wife and call her here by one of the popular aristocratic names of Syunik, Sopi [Sophi]. Legend says that this queen gave all her personal jewelry to the monastery of Tate.

SHAHANDUKHT

Grigor I Ashotian, the king of Syunik, reigned from 1044 to 1084. The wife of King Grigor, Shahandukht, was the daughter of the Aghvan king, Sevada. According to Stepanos Orbelian, Queen Shahandukht had no children. Queen Shahandukht and her sister Kata built the Church of the Holy Mother of God in

Vahanavank in the province of Dzork (Syunik) in 1086. After the death of her husband, Shahandukht took holy orders and lived as a hermit. She died in 1116.

But this is not the end of our story. Two queens of Syunik had the same name, Shahandukht: one of them was the wife of King Smbat I Sahakian, while the other one was the wife of Grigor I Ashotian. Historian Stepanos Orbelian claims that both were daughters of the king of Aghvan, Sevada. Orbelian writes:

"Smbat, son of Sahak, who was the son of Ashot, married Shahandukht, the daughter of the Aghvan prince Sevada." With this sentence, the author confirms Shahandukht was the wife of King Smbat.

In another chapter, Orbelian writes: "Grigor married the pious and deeply religious daughter of the great prince of the Aghvan kingdom, Sevada."

Since King Smbat (987–998) and King Grigor (1044–1084) reigned at different times, the two Shahandukhts could not have been sisters. Possibly there were two different princes or kings of Aghvan (or Artsakh) with the name Sevada, whose daughters had the same name, Shahandukht.

HRANUSH

King of Syunik, Senekerim Sevadian, reigned from 1084 to 1094. Stepanos Orbelian writes that King Senekerim donated the village of Arit to the monastery at Tate, and therefore issued an edict in which he mentioned by name many of his family members, including his sisters (Queen Shahandukht and Kata) and his sons (Grigor, Smbat, and Sevada).

But in that historical document, Senekerim did not mention his wife. Senekerim Sevada had also a daughter by the name Kata. We call his wife Hranush. It is possible that there was hostility between the king and the queen and this was the reason he did not include his wife's name in the edict.

MARIAM

The king of Syunik, Grigor II, succeeded his father, Senekerim, and reigned from 1103 to 1166. During the first years of his reign, the kingdom was actually ruled by the former king's sister, Queen Shahandukht.

There is no written evidence about the name of King Grigor's wife, so we will call her Mariam. Grigor and Mariam had only one daughter by the name of Kata. To keep the throne for a member of his family, Grigor ordered a young prince by the name of Hasan, brought from the aristocratic family of Khachen of Gerakar and married him to his daughter Kata. He declared Hasan the heir to the throne.

The historian of Syunik, Stepanos Orbelian, wrote nothing further about the wife of King Grigor I.

KATA

The king of Syunik, Hasan of Gerakar, reigned from 1166 to 1170.

His wife Kata was the daughter of King Grigor II. When the Turks occupied the fortress of Baghaberd (in 1170), Hasan with his family escaped to Khachen, which had been his home.

King Hasan and Kata had three sons, Vakhtang, Smbat, and Vasak.

MAMA

The king of Syunik, Hasan of Gerakar, after the death of his first wife Kata, married Mama or Mamkan, daughter of King Kyurike III. She was the sister of King Abas II.

Hasan of Gerakar and Queen Mama had three sons: Grigor, Khoydan, and Grigoris.

At the end of his life, Hasan Gerakaretsi distributed his possessions in Khachen among his six sons and entered the church. Hasan and Mama retired to the monastery of Dad, where Hasan's brother, Grigoris, was a priest.

CILICIAN KINGDOM

ZABLUN

Levon II Metsagorts ("of Great Accomplishments"), the founder of the Armenian kingdom of Cilicia, reigned from 1198 to 1219. In his first marriage, Levon took for his wife a woman named Zablun [Isabella], daughter of the prince of Antioch, Bohemond III. An Armenianized Frenchwomen, she had with King Levon II one daughter who was named Rita [also known as Stephanie].

Later, King Levon accused his wife of infidelity and had her locked up in the fortress of Vahka. Historians claim that the king's uncle Constantine, son of Vasak and the king's childhood companion, saved Zablun's life when King Levon began to beat her in the palace bedroom upon learning of her infidelity. If Constantine had not arrived in time, Levon would have killed her. After the imprisonment of the queen in Vahka fortress, the king sent his daughter Rita to live with his mother, Lady Rita. In 1215, Princess Rita was married to John of Brienne.

Queen Zablun died in the fortress of Vahka five years later. So great was the hostility of King Levon II that he had the queen buried without royal honors.

SIPIL

Upon the death of his first wife, King Levon II Metsagorts was married for the second time, in 1210, to Sipil [Sibylla], [65] sister of the king of Cyprus Hukon and daughter of Amery Lusignan of Cyprus. She was from the French branch of the family.

In 1216, Sipil gave birth to a daughter, Zabel, who was proclaimed heir to the Armenian throne by her father, King Levon II.

Zabel was the second woman in Armenian history to have been proclaimed ruler of the country, the first having been Queen Erato, the last representative of the Artashesian royal family.

After the death of Levon II, Prince Geoffrey, the lord of Sarvandikar Fortress, sought to marry Sipil so he could ascend the throne, but she decidedly rejected his offers. She moved away from the capital of Sis and settled in the fortress of Selevkia [Seleucia] in Isavria, where she lived with her French relatives. She returned in 1230 to be with her daughter Zabel, who had become by that time the queen of Cilician Armenia.

Sipil was always proud of her mother, Isabella Plantagenet, who was considered the most beautiful woman in the Lusignan family.

We do not know the date of Queen Sipil's death.

ZABEL

The queen of Cilician Armenia, Zabel, daughter of King Levon II Metsagorts, reigned from 1219 to 1222. In those years, she was still a young child and governed the kingdom with the help of guardians.

Earlier, in 1217, when the Fifth Crusade began, the East was invaded by European regiments led by the Austrian duke and the Hungarian king. The Armenians entered an alliance with the Hungarian king, Andreas. Levon II Metsagorts became friendly with King Andreas and the two kings agreed to the marriage of their children: the son of King Andreas, by the same name, was to marry the daughter of King Levon, Zabel. At that time, Zabel was only two years old and Andreas was eight. But they did not fulfill the agreement. The younger Andreas never came to Armenia, did not see Zabel, and later married a Venetian woman.

On April 7, 1223, the seven-year-old Zabel married the fourth son (Philip) of Bohemond IV, Duke of Antioch and Tripoli.

Philip, at that time, was seventeen years old. He turned out to be a big rogue. He governed Cilician Armenia with the help and influence of his father Bohemond and transported the Armenian treasury from Sis to Antioch. Philip and his father did not want to return the royal treasury and deceived the Armenians. In 1225, the Armenians dethroned and killed Philip. These times were very difficult for Queen Zabel.

Then Armenian princes married Zabel to Hetum, the son of her guardian Constantine. At first, Zabel refused her consent and escaped to her mother Sipil, in the fortress of Selevkia, where she was warmly received. But Constantine marched to the fortress and besieged it. The lord of the fortress, Bertran, was forced to hand over Queen Zabel to the Armenians. After returning to Sis, Zabel

81

was married to Hetum by Catholicos Kostantine Bardzrberdtsi on June 14, 1226, in the cathedral of Saint Sophia in Tarsus. Hetum, as the husband of Queen Zabel, was proclaimed king of Cilician Armenia and ruled until 1270.

In 1241, Queen Zabel ordered a hospital built in the capital city of Sis, where she and her daughters tended to poor patients. This was an important innovation, as there were no public hospitals in Europe then. On the front stone of this hospital was a plaque with the name of the queen and the date of construction.

Queen Zabel invited physicians from different parts of the kingdom to serve in the hospital. Not only did they treat patients, but they also prepared medications. Treatment in the hospital was free.

During the twenty-five years of Zabel's and Hetum's life together, they had eight children: three sons and five daughters. One son was Levon, heir to the throne; the second was Toros; and the third son, Ruben, died at three. One daughter, Isabel, also died young, at four. They named the other four daughters Fimi [Ephemia], Sipil [Sibylla], Rita, and Mariam [Maria]. Fimi was married to the prince of Sidon, Julien, at fourteen.

Queen Zabel died on her [thirty-sixth] birthday, on January 22, 1252. They buried her in the Drazark royal burial vault of the Rubinians.

KERAN

The king of Cilician Armenia, Levon III, reigned from 1270 to 1289. In 1262, he married Anna, daughter of the prince of Lambron, Hetum. Beginning in 1270, she was called Kir Anna, which meant "Mistress Anna," and before long, they shortened this name to Keran.

During twenty-one years of marriage, Levon III and Keran had fifteen children—eight sons and seven daughters (according to other sources, the couple had fourteen children). Queen Keran gave birth to more children than any other Armenian queen.

Two sons and two daughters died at an early age. The first daughter was born on April 4, 1263 and was named Zabel, after the king's mother. The first son, Hetum, was born on May 4, 1265. Then, daughter Fimi was born in 1266, daughter Sipil in 1269, son Toros in 1270, son Ruben in 1272, and daughter Zablun in 1274. In 1276, Queen Keran gave birth to twins, a boy and a girl.

In honor of the commander Smbat Sparapet, the boy was named Smbat, and the girl Sipil, which is another version of the name of Queen Zabel. In 1277, Keran gave birth to Prince Constantine. In 1278, she again gave birth to twins (daughters Rita and Teofane), in 1279 to Prince Nerses, and in 1283 another set of twins (sons Oshin and Alinakh).

In honor of his mother Zabel, King Levon named three of his daughters by related names—Zabel, Zablun, and Sipil. Five of the fifteen children, Hetum, Toros, Smbat, Constantine, and Oshin, later became the Armenian kings, though sometimes they battled against each other to gain the throne. These brothers were the only five king-brothers who succeeded each other to the Armenian throne. There are many words written in praise of Queen Keran. Her son Hetum claimed that "she had a wonderful soul and a beautiful body." It was said that "she is like a noble olive tie, bright and fertile." The chronicler Avetis described her as "a good friend to her husband in trouble and joy."

Most surprisingly, after having fifteen children, Keran became a nun and entered the Monastery of Drazark, assuming the name of Tevanna or Teolania, Queen Keran died on July 28, 1285, and is buried in Drazark.

MARGARITA

Hetum II, the king of Cilician Armenia, reigned from 1289 to 1296 and from 1209 to 1305. He was married to a Frenchwoman by the name of Margarita (Margaret).

In the absence of the king, his brother Smbat seized the throne, and in 1296, demanded that Queen Margarite leave the territory of Cilician Armenia within a few days.

Queen Margarita, however, did not go anywhere. On the first day of spring in the year 1296, she died suddenly.

MARGARITA

The king of Cilician Armenia, Toros I, reigned from 1294 to 1295. In 1285, he had married Margarita (Margaret), the daughter of the king of Cyprus, Hugon (Hugh),

Toros and Margarita had only one child, a son by the name of Levon, who later became king.

ZABEL

Smbat, the king of Cilician Armenia, reigned from 1296 to 1298. At nineteen, he had married the daughter of Guy of Ibelin (Jaffa), named Zabel (Isabella). Zabel's mother was Mariam, daughter of King Hetum I.

KHATUN

King Smbat had a second wife. After ascending the throne in 1296, he took a Mongol woman who was the great-granddaughter of Genghis Khan and the former wife of Smbat the Constable as his second wife. Smbat the Constable brought this Mongol woman from Mongolia, whose name was probably Khatun. [66]

It is possible that Smbat married Khatun, hoping to establish good relations with the Mongols and strengthening his power with their help. But Khatun was the Armenian queen for only two years (1296 to 1298) and probably had a hard life after King Smbat's downfall.

BEATRICHE

The king of Cilician Armenia, Constantine II, reigned from 1298 to 1299. We don't know the name of his wife and will call her Beatriche.[67] That name was popular in those times among the Cilician aristocrats. Probably this queen was Hellenic by origin, but we don't know whose daughter she was or from which family she was descended.

AGNES

Levon IV, son of Toros I and Margarita, reigned as king of Cilician Armenia from 1305 to 1307. In 1301 he had married Agnes,[68] the daughter of the sister of King Hetum II, Zablun. Agnes's father was Amorik [Amery], the brother of the king of Cyprus, Henry II. Hence, King Levon was married to his cousin (his father's sister's daughter). [69]

ZABLUN

The king of Cilician Armenia, Oshin I, reigned from 1308 to 1320. He was married to a woman by the name of Zablun (Isabella of Cyprus). She gave birth to their son, the future Levon V, in 1310 and died during labor.

HOVHANNA

After the death of his first wife, Oshin I married Hovhanna [Joanna, Jeanne of Anjou], who was also known as Irene, in 1316. She was the daughter of the prince of Sicily, Philip. After the death of Oshin I, Hovhanna married Prince Oshin [of Corycus], who was the bailiff of King Levon V.[70]

ALIS

Levon V, the king of Cilician Armenia, reigned from 1320 to 1342. At a very young age, he married the daughter of King Oshin, Alis [Alice]. King Levon suspected that his wife, who was much older than he, was deceiving him.

He accused her of infidelity and ordered her killed.

KOSTANDIA

After the violent death of his first wife, King Levon V in 1332 arranged a splendid wedding for his marriage to Kostandia [Constance] or, as she was also known, Eleonora, the daughter of the Sicilian king Frederik of Aragon. Eleanora was the widow of King Henry Il of Cyprus.

King Levon's sudden death in 1342 at thirty-two cut the conjugal life of Queen Eleanora short. King Levon did not have any children from either of his marriages.

KANDAKUZENIA

The king of Cilician Armenia Kvidon [Guy], or Constantine III, reigned from 1343 to 1344. King Constantine had earlier, in 1318, lived with his aunt, the Byzantine Empress Maria-Xenia (wife of Emperor Michael IX Palaeologus). At that time, the Byzantine emperor appointed Constantine as the governor of Pheris province in Macedonia and married him off to a daughter of Hovhannes Kandakuzen (John Cantacuzene). The Armenians killed King Constantine in Adana in 1344. The fate of his wife, whose name was probably Kondakuzenia after her father, is not known.

MARIUN

Constantine IV, King of Cilician Armenia, who was the son of Baldwin, lord of the fortress of Neghir, reigned from 1345 to 1363. He was married to Mariun (Maria or Marie), the daughter of Prince Oshin of Corcus and Queen Johanna.

Queen Mariun loved power and was a woman who had no qualms about the means used to achieve her ends. After the death of her husband, she tried to influence the new king, the son of Hetum, Constantine V. Unsuccessful in her efforts, she appealed to her uncle (her father's brother), Philip of Taranto titular Latin Emperor of Byzantium and to her grandfather Gregory, and asked them to replace King Constantine with a high-born European, hoping to become his wife.

On April 24, 1373, King Constantine V was killed and Queen Mariun was named interim ruler. She governed for fifteen months when, on July 26 of the next year, Levon VI Lusignan arrived.

In April 1375, the Mamelukes took Queen Mariun, along with Levon Lusignan, prisoner and sent them to Cairo. After being set free from captivity, Mariun went to Jerusalem, took holy orders, and spent her remaining days there, in the Armenian Monastery of Saint James.

MARGARITA

The king of Cilician Armenia Levon VI Lusinian [Lusignan] reigned for only seven months in 1374–1375. This last king of Cilician Armenia was the grandson of the king of Cyprus, Amery Lusignan, and Zabel, the daughter of Levon III. Their son (the father of King Levon VI) was named Jivan [John] and was married to Sultan [Soldana], daughter of the Georgian king.

Levon Lusignan married a Frenchwoman, Margarita (Margaret of Soissons, widow of the Cyprus prince Kandelion), in May 1369.

She was the daughter of Hovannes (John) of the Saxon royal family from the town of Famagusta.

In 1374, the Armenian senate offered Levon the throne of Cilician Armenia. With his wife and mother, he appeared in Corycus on Easter day—April 2, 1374. Then he set out for the capital of Sis, arriving there on July 26, 1374. He brought his mother and wife there a short time later.

In September 1374, Levon's wife Margarita gave birth to twin daughters, who were named Mariam and Katariné. Margarita had another daughter from her first husband, Prince Kandelion, by the name of Phenna. Phenna was twelve years old when Margarita married Levon, and she came with them to Corycus. There she met the young prince of Corcus, Shahan, and was engaged to him. Their wedding took place in Sis.

On September 14, 1374, in the Church of Saint Sophia in Sis, Levon Lusignan was proclaimed king of Cilician Armenia. After he ascended the throne, he appointed the Latin leader Mateus de Shapp as the chief of the court—or in today's terminology, the prime minister of the kingdom—and married the widow of King Constantine (son of Hetum).

In 1375, the Mamluks invaded Cilician Armenia and on April 22 they captured King Levon and his family (including Queen Margarita and her children). the prince of Corcus Shahan, and Queen Mariun, the widow of King Constantine IV (son of Baldwin).

Queen Margarita and her twin daughters, Mariam and Katariné, could not tolerate life in Cairo in captivity. The twins became ill and died in 1379, and Queen Margarita in 1381. They burried Queen Margarita in the courtyard of the Armenian Church of Saint Minas in Cairo.

Levon VI Lusignan spent many years in captivity after the death of his wife and daughters and eventually was liberated with the help of European monarchs. He died on November 29, 1393, and was buried in a church in Paris. They moved his white marble tombstone to the royal burial-vault in Saint Denis after the French Revolution. The tombstone is intact, but the king's remains, along with other royal remains, were disinterred and dispersed during the French Revolution.

INDEX

Hutomia (wife of Mehruzhan Ervanduni) 26

Hutomia (wife of Tigran II) 33

Hutsan 14

Janama 38

Kandakuzenia 85

Kaputan 14

Kata (wife of Abusahl-Hamazasp Artsruni) 71

Kata (wife of Hasan of Syunik) 78
Katranidé (wife of Ashot I) 64
Katranidé (wife of Smbat Bagratuni) 67

Katranidé (wife of Gagik I) 67

Keran 82

Khatun 84

Khorsovanush (wife of Khosrov I) 49
Khosrovanuvsh (wife of Ashot III) 67
Khushush 72

Knkush 61

Kostandia 85

Koton 11

Kupghidukht 76

Lusatikin 26

Mama 78

Mamkan 74

Margarita (wife of Hetum IT) 83
Margarita (wife of Toros I) 83
Margarita (wife of Levon VT) 86
Mariam (wife of Abas Bagratunis 66

Mariam (wife of Grigor Il of Syunik) 77

Mariun 86

Maya 44

Mazeta 48

Mihrana 19

Mlké 70

Morch 26

Naira 7

Nané 22

Nazenik 47

Nersehanuysh 51

Nushik 50

Octava 39

Olympia 57

Orash 11

Parandzem 54

Parisuhi 73

Patar 13

Romela 58

Rusaina 10

Ruzukan 75

Sahakanuysh 66

Samosia 24

Sandukht 46

Sasa 38

Sahandukht 50

Satenik 30

Seda 75

Shahandukht (wife of Smbat I of Syunik) 75

[1] *In ancient times in rural areas, daughters did not have proper names and were referred to by the names of their fathers, e.g., Vruyr's daughter. In the present, this tradition exists in some remote villages where, in conversation, a girl may be referred to by her father's name.*

[2] *In 1968, during the celebration of Yerevan's 2750th anniversary, I witnessed the following conversation between two historians:*
"If we start from the cuneiform manuscript of Argishti discovered on Arinbera Hill, then means water, river, or sea."
The well-known expert in cuneiform, Hovhannes Karageozian, has theorized that five and a half thousand years ago the name of the city of Yerevan was Kodon, taken from the name of the Koton River, meaning "sea river," because it originated from the small sea of Sevan.

[3] *In the remote past, the Armenians had a tradition of naming their beloved wives by the names of Armenian rivers. Presumably, by naming his wife Koton, Rusa II expressed his great and passionate love for her. (By the way, the word "ton" in contemporary Armenian is used to refer to a heavy rain or downpour.)*

[4] *Xenophon, History of Cyrus, see Readings in the History of the Armenian People (Yerevan, 1981), p. 139.*

[5] *Units of the Armenian infantry and cavalry fought with the Persian King Darius, who was defeated by Alexander the Great in this battle—Editor.*

[6] *Not to be confused with Mount Nemrut near the western shores of Lake Van in the Bznunik province.*

[7] *(The reference here is apparently to the account by historian Movses Khorenatsi regarding the beheading of Ervand IV following the king's defeat in the rebellion that brought his successor, King Artashes, to the throne. See Moses Khorenatsi: History of the Armenians, with Translation and Commentary by Robert W. Thomson (Harvard University Press: Cambridge, 1978), pp. 184-87—Editor.)*

[8] *History of the Armenian People, vol. 1 (Yerevan: Armenian Academy of Sciences 1971), pp. 512- 13.*

[9] *Armosata was the capital of Isopk, Arshamasht.*

[10] *Mihrdat was the son of the sister of Antiochus III and an Armenian prince. In 201 BC, he was assigned by Antiochus as the governor of Little Armenia (Pokr Hayk).*

[11] *Beautiful Field is the valley of Aratsani and is known also as the field of Kharberd.*

[12] *Readings in the History of the Armenian People, p. 192.*

[13] *In literary Armenian, the word "morch" means the branch of a young tree.*

[14] *Cyril Toumanoff, Armenian Inscription (Venice, 1970), p. 25.*

[15] *(The English translations are taken from Robert W. Thomson, Movses Khorenatsi, pp 192–93—Editor.)*

[16] *Hutomia or Hutohma in the Parthian language is formed from the words hu (well) and tohma (birth, origin, family, generation) and means "well-born" or "high-born."*

[17] *Vardan Hatsuni, The Armenian Woman Before History (Venice, 1936), p. 416.*

[18] See his book, Extensive History from the Origins of Armenia to Present Days (Boston: Yeran Press, 1917).

[19] *Readings in the History of the Armenian People, p. 283.*

[20] *In the thirty-seventh book of his work, History of Rome.*

[21] *Upon his ascension to the throne, Artashes I avenged his father's death by ordering the massacre of the Roman garrisons found in Armenia. He was assassinated in 20 BC. See Nina Garsoian, "The Emergence of Armenia," in The Armenian People from Ancient to Modern Times, edited by Richard G. Hovannisian, vol. 1 (New York: St. Martin's Press, 1997), p. 61—Editor.)*

[22] *Tigran the Great (Antilias, 1947), p. 7.*

[23] *The Downfall of Artashesian Wealth (Beirut, 1967), p. 153.*

[24] *Readings in the History of the Armenian People, p. 317.*

[25] *Electra is the name of a Greek goddess, the daughter of Ovkianos (Ocean) and Tetis.*

[26] *Zenobia is a Greek word meaning someone who has divine power.*

[27] *An account of these events can be found in Tacitus: The Annals of Imperial Rome, translated with an Introduction by Michael Grant: (New York: Penguin Books, 1978), p. 272–73—Ed.*

[28] *Readings in the History of the Armenian People, vol. 1, pp. 327–28. [The English version is taken from Tacitus: The Annals of Imperial Rome, Translated by Michael Grant, P. 275.]*

[29] *See H. Acharian, Dictionary of Armenian Proper Names, vol. 2, pp. 205–6.*

[30] *Arianos is quoted in H. Manandian, Critical Theory of the History of the Armenian People, vol. 2, part I (Yerevan, 1957), p. 15; Khorenatsi is in History of the Armenians (Yerevan, 1940, p. 106.*

[31] *History of the Armenians, p. 152.*

[32] *Acharian, Dictionary of Armenian Proper Names, vol. 1, p. 179.*

[33] *History of the Armenians (Yerevan, 1977), p. 136.*

[34] *[The sources provide contradictory information regarding the circumstances, dates, and order of Arshak's two marriages—Editor.]*

[35] *History of the Armenians, p. 204. [English translation in Thomson, pp. 292–93.]*

[36] *[History of the Armenians, pp 191–94. The English translation is based on that found in Robert W. Thomson, Moses Khorenatsi, pp. 276–80.*

[37] *Pavstos Buzand, History of the Armenians (Yerevan, 1968), pp. 168–70, 172, 174, 220. [The English translation is taken from The Epic Histories Attributed to Pawstos Buzand, translation and commentary by Nina G. Garsoian (Cambridge: Harvard University Press, 1989), pp. 140–44, 176.]*

[38] *History of the Armenians, p. 174; [the English translation is from Garsoian, Pawstos Buzand, p. 145].*

[39] *Armenian Woman Before History, p. 52.*

[40] *History of the Armenians, pp. 193–94; [Thomson, Khorenatsi, pp. 276, 280.]*

[41] *Acharian, Dictionary of Armenian Proper Names, vol. 4, p. 186. [Garsoian, in Pawstos Buzand, gives the date of Olympia's marriage to Arshak as 358—Editor.]*

[42] *Pavstos Buzand, History of the Armenians (Yerevan, 1968), p.283; (Garsoian,*

Pavstos Buzand, p. 221.
[43] *Armenian Woman Before History, p. 91.*
[44] *History of the Armenians, p. 393; [Garsoian, Pavstos Buzand, p. 228].*
[45] *Buzand, History of the Armenians, p. 282; [Garsoian, Pavstos Buzand, p. 228].*
[46] *Buzand, History of the Armenian, p. 298; [Garsoian, Pavstos Buzand, p. 233].*
[47] *History of the Aghvan World (Yerevan, 1969), pp. 45, 28, 62.*
[48] *Makar Barkhudarian, History of Aghvan, vol. 1 (1900), p. 164.*
[49] *The name Katranide is an Armenian version of the European name, Katherine. The diminutive of the name Katranidé is Kata.*
[50] *History of the Armenian People, vol. 3 (Yerevan, Armenian Academy of Sciences, 1976), p. 22*
[51] *Acharian, Dictionary of Armenian Proper Names, vol. 2, p. 538.*
[52] *History of Syunik (Yerevan, 1986), p. 259.*
[53] *[Quoted by Nina Garsoian, "The Independent Kingdoms of Medieval Armenia," in The Armenian People from Ancient to Modern Times, Hovannistian, ed., vol. 1, p. 180—Editor.]*
[54] *Armenian Woman Before History, p. 169.*
[55] *Acharian, Dictionary of Armenian Proper Names, vol. 4, pp. 34, 181.*
[56] *Acharian, Dictionary of Armenian Proper Names, vol. 2, p. 266; vol. 3, pp. 365–66*
[57] *Aristakes Lastivertsi, History (Yerevan, 1971), p. 12.*
[58] *Dictionary of Armenian Proper Names, vol. 2, p. 562.*
[59] *Armenian Woman Before History, p. 169.*
[60] *History of the Armenian People, vol. 3, p. 97.*
[61] *Acharian, Dictionary of Armenian Proper Names, vol. 1, p. 435,*
[62] *Ibid., vol. 3, p. 187.*
[63] *The name Seda originated from the Arabian word seyda, which means "the mistress" ("sovereign"). This name is used also in our days.*
[64] *Acharian, Dictionary of Armenian Proper Names, vol. 4, p. 331.*
[65] *According to H. Acharian, the name Sipil is a French word of Greek origin. It was popular among Armenians in thirteenth and fourteenth centuries.*
[66] *See Hatsuni, Armenian Woman Before History, p. 53.*
[67] *Beatriche in Latin means "happy."*
[68] *Agnes is a Greek word that means "pure."*
[69] *Alishan, Sisuan, p. 543.*
[70] *Acharian, Dictionary of Armenian Proper Names, vol. 3, p. 537*

www.ingramcontent.com/pod-product-compliance
Lightning Source LLC
Chambersburg PA
CBHW020809020726
47495CB00008B/2656